IT WAS A *TANTO*, THE SAMURAI DAGGER, USED TO BEHEAD THE ENEMY.

The Figure was doing his damnedest to make sure it served its traditional purpose, but the months between their confrontations had not slowed Daremo. His head moved. The blade went by his neck and stuck into the tree behind him. It sank five inches into the bark meat.

Daremo was already rolling to his left side, desperately trying to keep his hands from reaching for the *shurikens* he knew were not there.

The Figure's arms shot out like hydraulic pistons, trying to break through Daremo's preliminary defenses, trying to batter ribs, break septum, stop heart...

Daremo shot up, leaping in place in the air. The Figure shot his fingers toward the leaping man. Daremo grabbed the outstretched arm, giving himself a vaulting-off point. Using the Figure's arm like a branch, Daremo threw himself over the Figure's head.

The Figure kicked his right leg up. An incredible kick, straight up. The leg went out, as if the Figure were kicking a football, but then it just kept going until the straight leg was bent all the way against the Figure's chest. His foot connected with Daremo's face as he was about to swing his legs to the ground...

THE YEAR OF THE NINJA series
by Wade Barker

Dragon Rising
Lion's Fire
Serpent's Eye
Phoenix Sword*

Published by
WARNER BOOKS

*forthcoming

SERPENT'S EYE

The Year of the Ninja Master: Autumn

Wade Barker

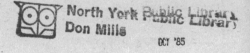

WARNER BOOKS

A Warner Communications Company

As usual, all places, all legend, and all lore actually exist. Even the mental shenanigans are possible. Of course only Wade Barker is a total figment of your fevered imaginations. Dipotassium phosphate, mono- and diglycerides (for uniform dispersion of oil), tripotassium citrate (aids dissolving), silicon dioxide (prevents caking), and tetrasodium pyrophosphate.

WARNER BOOKS EDITION

Cover design by Gene Light

Warner Books, Inc.
75 Rockefeller Plaza
New York, N.Y. 10019

 A Warner Communications Company

Printed in the United States of America

First Printing: September, 1985

10 9 8 7 6 5 4 3 2 1

TO WHITLEY STRIEBER

"I have a bumblebee in my mouth."

Acknowledgment

To Frank Bender, Kenneth Musante, and all the other mercenaries: another kind of will power.

Part One

With curious art the brain, too finely
   wrought,
Preys on herself, and is destroyed
   by thought.

                    Charles Churchill

1

Blood.

You live with it. It *is* you. You take it for granted—even when it dribbles from a cut.

But too much blood sends a signal. You can feel it even if you can't see it. Fear is the signal.

Think of it as a wave. A tidal wave, a *tsunami* over your soul.

Fear is like a serpent inside you. A serpent that chases its tail all the time. When it catches it, and makes that circle inside you, that's when you feel mortality. Death will come. You realize one day you *just won't wake up*, and you look the serpent right in the eye.

Daremo sat down. Hard. His whole body shook as his ass hit the moss-covered rocks. The air was thin and the sky stretched all around him. He could see forever unless he turned to face the clouds below him. The fluffy white plowlike clouds made forever's floor up here.

He smiled in joy. The beauty of this place, its wonder, made him enjoy even the pain. At least it wasn't someplace squalid, where his death would seem meaningless. Here, his death was beautiful, even if its cause was unnatural.

It was hard to believe in the face of all this magnificence that tiny balls of lead could rip out his lights, hard to believe that mere bullets could take him from this. And maybe at the same time make him part of this ethereal world too. But they could. They were in the process of doing it at that very moment. It was happening fast. Daremo's life was measured in moments now.

He wanted to drink in the magnificence—he tried to, even as he felt it all falling apart inside him. The bullets were doing their ugly work. They ripped apart everything between his heart and his manhood. Three or four good ones right in the gut cutting all those important lines, chopping down all the connections to the power supply and the big boss upstairs.

The power supply was stupid. It kept pumping all the good stuff out into the cut lines. The big boss saw it happening and screamed with all its might, but the power supply kept pumping. Pretty soon the stuff that was keeping the boss running would pass through and spill out too.

The boss was running out of time, so it did what any good boss would do. It separated the moments, analyzed, organized, and summarized them.

Then it waited for the end.

Daremo sat in the room without walls, without a
ceiling, with clouds for a floor, dying. They had shot
him in the stomach three or four times. He sat down
hard. He didn't have the strength to continue. It took
all his strength to die.

This was the fourth time.

Brian Williams had died to become the Ninja Master.
He killed the men who had mutilated his loved ones—
born and unborn—and went to the Orient to hide out.

In the Orient, he learned what is laughingly called
ninjutsu—a real hip, with-it martial art that sells. He
came back to America as Brett Wallace, a swaggering,
high-living, do-gooding asshole who went to the best
bistros with the most beautiful women.

Then his masters in the Orient yanked him back to
school to teach him the way it really worked. These
were ninjas, for God's sake, *real* ninjas—the ones that
killed for a living.

They kept him in the Orient for years learning the
way of their world. Ninjas were a family, like the Cosa
Nostra. You don't screw around with them, wearing
stupid black costumes and throwing metal stars into
eyeballs. You wear whatever outfit gets you where you
want to go and poison the damn star so a scratch
anywhere will do the job.

The job is killing. For ninjas, their killing talents
were for hire or to secure the family. But for their own
reasons, they gave Wallace all their murderous knowledge and let him go back to the States. But he had had

to "die" a second time for that. On the occasion of his rebirth, they had presented him with his swords—the soul of the warrior.

Once home, Wallace did not find the killing easy. He murdered murderers, rapists, and other criminals. Even if all his killing had done any good, he still would have gone nuts. As it was, the uselessness of all the killing only made his insanity that much greater, darker, more all-encompassing when it finally came.

Daremo couldn't tell this to anybody. Not because he was dying, but because he doesn't remember. He died a third time, then, when he went insane. This is the end of his fourth life. A real, physical death this time. The other deaths were psychological but no less real. The third death destroyed Brett Wallace, and Daremo was born.

Dare mo is Japanese for "nobody." That's who the Ninja Master is now. The ultimate ninja: nobody.

I've been here before, Daremo thought. *The room with no walls, no floor, no ceiling. I go here every time I lose consciousness or go off the deep end. I go here trying to understand.*

I went all over the world trying to find a tangible image for the spot. Is this it? Or am I dreaming now?

I am shot. I know that.

I should have learned by now. There's no way to distinguish between reality, subterfuge, psychic war, and lunch with the gods. That's what I call it. I dream, and I see the gods.

At least I don't have to fight them. I have to fight

everything else. Ever since San Francisco, I've had to achieve something on the psychic level before I could achieve something on a physical plane. I had to defeat something in my mind before I could fight tangible things.

What do I know? I know something happened in San Francisco. I had visions. That's something more than nightmares or hallucinations. I had those too, but they became the more realistic visions. I was being psychically attacked by outside forces. Probably the Chinese. The Moshuh Nanren.

It was the Chinese Moshuh Nanren—the "magic men," the forerunners of the ninja. The Chinese had brainwave weapons. They attacked me with them. Jerks. They attacked before they knew what they were doing. No big surprise there. How many people use guns without knowing how they work?

Ha, ha. They blew a hole in my mind. The stuff I never used came roaring into the stuff I do use. Human beings use something like ten to twenty-five percent of their brains. Now I'm using some more.

We're all dying. What are we alive for? No answers in that other seventy-five percent of the brain.

The Japanese had it covered. The samurai lived in preparation to die. That was Bushido, the "way of the warrior." But Bushido was based on a lousy premise. But they had the code, and to question the code was to destroy the code, so they ignored its bullshit base. Instead, they tried to seal the base's cracks. The ninja was the mortar.

Ninja did all the dirty work, took care of all the

problems the Bushido *didn't allow the samurai to face.
But the bullshit just rolled on.* Bushido *said that the
ninjas were less than scum of the earth for doing the
things they had to do* because *of* Bushido. *So the ninja
suffered because of all the emotions that* Bushido *didn't
take into account. Like pride. Human pride.*

I'm dying.

*I don't have time to waste. There are only a few
seconds left to understand what happened to me.
Understand who I am, what I am.*

Brian Williams couldn't understand what led the
motorcycle gang members to kill his wife, parents, and
unborn child. He was driven mad by it. He became
Brett Wallace. Brett Wallace couldn't understand why
he killed dozens of people. He was driven mad by it.
He became Daremo. He had to become Daremo because Daremo didn't care.

Daremo didn't care why he killed or why others
killed. He accepted that human beings killed other
human beings and that they often didn't have anything
resembling good reasons for it. He accepted that he
killed for reasons maybe others wouldn't think were
good. He didn't care, so he didn't go mad.

He was *ki-chigaino*—the Japanese walking crazy. These
were the insane who accepted their insanity and lived
within it. The only clue to their insanity was who they
were and everything they did.

Daremo remembered the nightmares of his birth. He
remembered the fleeting scenes of his earlier Williams/
Wallace life—the violent scenes, the death he had

witnessed and caused in his previous two lives. He could understand those now, at least. His mind had been torn by the *Moshuh Nanren* psychic attacks. They created new channels in his mind. But when a mind was exploded, it didn't all fit back into place like a magnetized puzzle.

When he tried to understand the violence, his recuperating mind showed him the images: of corpses tearing open and spilling insects, which tore him apart; of corpses *turning into* giant insects, which tried to attack him. His mind had become a meteorological station, picking up human weather forecasts from all over the Daremo universe.

His mind went on from there. It gingerly showed him new ways to think. It introduced new processes, which were to become as automatic and unconscious as breathing. But to someone who had never breathed before, breathing would be a shock and an effort.

But Daremo's was a violent life, a life already crammed with horror. To teach a murderer to utilize his suprahumanity required even more mental gymnastics. Daremo was assailed by images, and the part of his mind that he was accustomed to labored to organize and present them.

Daremo also remembered the moment of his birth. He was lying on his bed in San Francisco. A figure in black was standing over him, trying to push a sword into his chest. To a newly born warrior, it was life.

Daremo fought the figure in black—*the* Figure in Black—and escaped when the ceiling fell in. The bed he had been lying on was soon consumed by flames.

The Figure escaped, and Daremo's three "parents" lay unconscious on the floor.

Daremo remembered them as he walked away: Jeff Archer, his student and friend, Brett Wallace had helped him. Rhea Tagashi, his lover. A beautiful Oriental woman, and the only blood member of the ninja family that had adopted him. Shiban Kan Hama, a friend, and, as it turned out, Daremo's guardian from the *ninja ryu* (school).

They were no longer important. The Figure in Black had attacked him. *That* was important. The Figure in Black was not a petty thief, a miserable rapist, a disgusting murderer. He was the Figure in Black. He was a key to why Daremo was.

The Figure in Black attacked from a previous existence that had had no purpose. To Brett Wallace's horror, even a life killing killers had no purpose. Then out of the tortured images came the sword, the extension of the Figure's very soul—if samurai dictum had *any* validity. It sought to abort Daremo's life, his purpose. It didn't, so Daremo sought to discover that purpose.

There's an old feudal ninja tale. A warlord's minions were chasing one of the assassin/spies. They followed him to a small village. They saw him running toward a group of old people. The elderly village citizens were out for a walk. The ninja ran toward the group. The warlord's guards moved in.

But when the ninja reached the old people, he disappeared. He ran into the group but never emerged. Try as they might, the guards could find no sign of the young, robust ninja. The old people walked on, seemingly oblivious of the drama and the soldiers' confusion. The men returned to their warlord's castle to report their failure and commit seppuku.

From this incident grew legends of ninja invisibility. In fact, it is the legend of the ninja's true art—the art of infiltration. The ninja *became* an old man. He was so expert in the human process—both physical and mental— that he practically changed himself into an elderly villager.

The highest achievement of a martial artist is to defeat one's opponent without physical contact. The highest achievement of a ninja is the ability to actually become someone else. Until that time, Daremo had to be satisfied with infiltrating, blending in with, this brave new world while he sought to make sense of his birth.

For that, for all of it, he would need money. To track the Figure in Black, to fight the forces behind his opponent, to have the freedom and security to learn the techniques needed to become others, he would need money, lots of money. Quickly.

Daremo walked away from Brian Williams and Brett Wallace. He walked away from Jeff Archer, Rhea Tagashi, and Shiban Kan Hama. He went out into the brave new world to make his fortune.

2

Deep, cool, and light—that was the night. The sun was on the other side of the world. America had turned its back on it, plunging itself into the star-studded ink of eternal space. But the East Coast held up candles instead of cursing, infusing the air with its own yellow borealis. Outside, there was no place that was truly dark.

The air held more than light. It held a brisk coolness, a slightly damp chill that stroked the skin rather than clamping onto the bones. It was a coolness one could almost taste.

Daremo sat on the side of the road, just where the street curved between two diners, and indulged his senses. This was a powerfully beautiful world, a place to be savored. It was just too bad everybody was *ki-chigaino*.

Just look at the town. If Daremo took five steps to his

left, he could gaze down a straightaway lined with a useless bounty. On the right side of the road, snuggling uncomfortably close to each other, were an empty produce stand and a boarded-up take-out restaurant. A single sign was left inside the dirty windows of the empty establishment: HOT DOGS BOILED IN BEER.

On the left side of the road was the Blue Sky Diner. The old neon sign out front said the BLU KY DI ER to the dark. Next to that was another restaurant, the Boardwalk. Beyond that, the highway, a magnificent monstrosity on eight legs. It was pale blue in the night, lit up with bright yellow-orange lights.

If Daremo went five steps to the right, there'd be another straightaway and a four-way stop with a traffic light. On the right side was a Greek diner. Next to that was a gas station. It used to be a family-run place—with the name of the manager in the window and a three-door bay—where nearby residents could get friendly repair work and passing tourists could be taken for a ten-percent markup. But now the garage was boarded up in preparation for tearing down and the full service became self-service.

Across the street was a *shopter*, a mini-shopping center. It had been a full-fledged shopping center before the giant malls had become the norm, then some wisenheimer in the town hall coined the phrase *shopter*. It had parking space for about eight cars and only two stores that motorists remembered. They were the brightly lit laundromat and the pizza parlor.

No one could ever remember what the third, tiniest store was, so it became whatever the times deemed hip. It had been a head shop, a T-shirt shop and, most recently, a candy/videogame hangout, but even that was closed and dark now.

Next to it was a club, a combination pizza restaurant and dance hall called Mister B's. It was a singles' hangout and, considering the quality of singles in the Stratford area, not the most respectable of places. The town cops could gauge the arrest potential of a place by the number of motorcycles and steel-blue cars on super-shocks in the lot. Mr. B's had a goodly percentage.

The street was made for eating. Five open restau-rants in a row—only the beer-dogs having failed in that small, bending section of Connecticut. But Daremo wasn't hungry. He rose from his sitting position with a certain pomp. Daremo was here because of Brett Wallace.

Wallace had been working feverishly before he "died." He had seen and felt his death coming and wanted to prepare whoever came after him. He leased post office boxes and bank safety-deposit boxes. He even buried information and money around San Francisco for his successor to find. With all the materials available to Brett Wallace the Ninja Master, he put together a personal financial plan for Daremo.

Brett Wallace had the deus ex machina computer that was handily hooked up to most of the heavy-duty computer networking throughout the country. Wallace could do research up the wazoo. When Wallace's fancy bachelor pad and wardrobe of clothes went up in na-palm, Daremo was sent out naked into the world. But Daddy had left an inheritance. Some money . . . not nearly enough . . . some ideas, and some names.

Daremo walked across the street and toward the intersection, leaving the highway behind. His walking stick clicked on the decaying asphalt as he went. That's the way the *ki-chigaino* built it. They laid the road down every spring, let the tires chew it up every summer, let the cool fall contract the wounds, and let the winter make the potholes.

Daremo stood at the corner, to the right of Mr. B's. The road that intersected the pock-marked street was wide, with four lanes. To the north, it stretched hundreds of yards until it disappeared over a slight incline. To the south, it extended to the curling highway and, beyond that, the Atlantic Ocean.

The pock-marked street was industrial, filled with eateries, gas stations, and the like. The four-lane road was residential, with beautiful three-story houses that must have been charming before the arrival of the diners. The area was a big cross; one part unstained by time, handsome, the other a growing cancerous blight of baklava, mozzarella cheese, and ninety-two octane unleaded.

Daremo turned his back on the bubbling pepperoni blight. It had its place, but not tonight. Tonight was for the neatly manicured grass, held in place by the late October cold. Tonight was for the ancient trees, giant, bark-covered lawn jockies for the vaguely Victorian houses. Tonight was for the homes and the two or three families that lived in each of them.

Stratford used to be a place just for the motorcycle and steel-blue super-shock men who couldn't afford to live anyplace else except Bridgeport or Norwalk—but wouldn't be caught dead there because there were "too many niggers." But now the working joe moved in too, took care of the long line of big, rambling houses the cycle guys didn't know what to do with.

Some people, when you give them more than a hovel, start wrecking the place to create a hovel. The landlords took the expansive homes away from these jerks, happy to sell them to growing families and responsible lower-middle-class joes. It was a new postwar era, an era no one talked about—not like the one immediately after World War II and, to some slight degree, the Korean conflict.

The Vietnam vets bought the houses. They had readjusted and married and had kids. They needed someplace to live and Uncle Sam gave them diddly-squat to do it. So they couldn't buy the nineteen-thousand-dollar home in the chi-chi areas of Monroe or Redding as had their predecessor vets in 1952. They were left to fend for themselves in 1978 Norwalk, Bridgeport, Stratford, or the valley—the once-proud industrial towns of Derby and Ansonia, now an empty gray.

They did all right, though. They had the working-class values that made America great. They had fought for their country, no matter how stupid the cause. Or, more accurately, no matter how untenable the situation.

Daremo took a left and ambled down the street past Mr. B's.

Across the four-lane road, on the second floor of the second house from the corner, Scott Harmon stood at his brother-in-law's butcher block kitchen table. "You do what I told you to?" he asked his sister-in-law as she walked in.

"Yeah, Scott," she said with mild irritation, helping Sally through the doorway. "Don't say hello or nothing."

"Hello," he said.

"Hello, Uncle Scott," Sally said with intense pleasure.

"Hello, darling," Scott said to her, moving his head to look at the eight-year-old. "You do all right tonight?"

"Great!" the child boomed. Considering the evening, her response could only be called greedy.

"Thank God Halloween only comes once a year," her mother, Wendy, said with relief, hanging up her little witch-daughter's coat.

"I got a lot of candy!" Sally announced, holding the bag up to Scott as her father, Mark, came into the room. She instantly swung it toward her dad as he went to the fridge, an empty beer bottle in his hand.

"That's great, dear," he said casually as he dug another beer out and threw the empty into the plastic trashcan behind Scott. "You coming in to watch the movie, Scott?" he asked.

"Yeah." He leaned down and pulled a mini-Oh Henry bar from Sally's tearing fingers. "Not yet, honey. In a second."

"You gonna eat candy?" she asked, her *hey, this is my booty* tone unmistakable.

"No, dear. Just going to look it over," Scott said, putting a meaty hand on her tiny shoulder. "Come on in. We'll watch the movie and show everybody what you got."

"They gonna eat candy?" Sally asked timidly.

"No, dear, it's all yours," Mark said, a smile growing beneath his moustache. "We just want to see." He was leaning against the sink counter, holding his fresh beer.

"I did great, Daddy!" she gushed. "Really good."

"Come on," Scott said, and they all went into the living room. Scott's pregnant wife was there, as was her best friend, Carol. They both said things like, "Hey, how did it go?" and "Watcha got there?"

The room was long and comfortable. All the walls were bright beige. The three windows behind the couch were shaded by clean yellow drapes. The wall-to-wall carpet was off-white. The furniture was tweedy, more designer-trendy than Scott's catalog-bought furniture upstairs. The TV was a color twenty-five-inch floor jobber. It was alive with the image of Anthony Hopkins.

Scott sat down next to his wife on the couch and poured the candy out of Sally's bag. Mark frowned, thinking that should have been Sally's prerogative. But the little girl didn't seem to mind. Her eyes glowed as the goodies spilled out.

Mr. Goodbars, Snickers, M & M's, Baby Janes, Tootsie Rolls, Heath Bars, Fifth Avenues, Schraffts, and all the other stuff came pouring across the simple coffee table. Almost all of them were the mini-bars, the version bought in supermarket bags. Only a few were the standard full-size bars you could get at the candy counter.

"Oh, Scott," his wife exclaimed as some candy slipped over the edges onto the carpet. Scott picked up the stuff on his side while Sally gathered the stuff on hers.

She held it in her pudgy little hands until Scott asked her to put it with the main pile.

Only Carol watched the movie, *Audrey Rose*. The others looked at the candy. To Sally's eyes, it was just candy, the same as all the stuff her friends had gotten. But the others could clearly see the markings. On each wrapper, no matter how small the piece, there was a number Sally's mother had written with a felt-tip pen. Scott picked a Mounds mini-bar and looked at it. There was a number five on it.

"Let's do it in order," Scott's wife suggested.

"No," Mark moaned, spread out in his easy chair, looking over the table toward the television.

"What, put the pieces in order? By number?" Mark's wife said in disbelief. "What for?"

"I'll just check them," Scott said quietly, already sifting through. He picked up every piece, looked it over carefully, then dropped it back into the bag as Sally stared silently. He checked the wrappings' seams. As he studiously continued his work, all eyes slowly turned toward him, like those of an audience watching a high-wire act. They wanted the acrobat to fall but hoped he didn't. Scott paused, looking at one candy bar he held above his head.

"What is it, Scott?" his wife asked intently.

He didn't answer for a second. "Nothing," he then said, dropping the bar into the bag. Everyone emitted an audible sigh of relief. Sally's smile had disappeared when the question had been asked but returned when the answer came.

As the process went on, eyes returned to the television set. Even Sally's eyes. She didn't even ask if she could eat the candy Scott had put back into the bag. When she had first gotten in, she was candy mad. But since then she had adjusted to the serious tone. The thrill of the prizes was still there, but the desire to devour them was momentarily restrained.

No one noticed at first when Scott carefully put down a Mars Almond bar and took the folded piece of paper out of his back pocket. His wife noticed when he put the unfolded sheet on the coffee table.

"What is it?" she asked nervously. When he didn't answer, she repeated the question. Scott refolded the paper and put it away.

"I'll be right back," he said, suddenly getting up and walking toward the kitchen door, pulling his blue jacket off the coat rack as he went.

"Scott!" his wife called with a hint of fear.

Mark picked up the candy bar. A glob of gray glue rubbed against his finger as he felt the seam. Rubber cement. Mark tore open the candy bar.

"Daddy!" Sally complained, her stockpile compromised.

"Just a second, honey." Mark looked the candy bar over, then tore it in half. The business end of a simple pin, the kind that comes in department-store shirts, was revealed to the soft white light of the living room.

Mark caught up with Scott halfway down the back stairs. "Wait up, will you? Let the police handle this."

Scott had instructed Mark's wife to have a second goody bag, which she would hold while Sally trick-or-treated. At every house, Mark's wife would mark the candy given to Sally with a number before pouring it into the second goody bag. That way, Sally went up to each house with an empty goody bag. Scott had the "key"—the numbering system—in his back pocket.

"What are they going to do?" Scott asked. "Fine him?"

"They'll put him in jail," Mark promised.

"How long?" Scott asked, and marched outside.

Scott's wife appeared at the top of the stairs. "Mark!" she wailed.

"Take it easy," he said, turning, holding his hands up. "He'll be all right."

"I don't want him to get in any trouble!"

"Come on, Elaine," Mark said tensely. "You know Scott."

Daremo saw Scott Harmon walking across the street. He could see clearly in his face and manner what the man was planning to do. There was no mistaking the lynch look. Daremo moved casually but quickly down the walk, until he neared the man. Scott had stopped in front of a house as a twelve-year-old came down the steps. It was a place diagonally across the street from Harmon's, three driveways down.

"What did ya get?" Scott asked, his lips wide. "Mars Bar?"

"Yeah," the kid answered, almost as if saying, *What's it to you, pervert? Care to make anything of it?*

Scott walked by him. The kid walked on. By the time he reached the front porch, Harmon was running. He took the steps in a single jump and banged his fist on the door once as his other hand twisted around the knob. He threw the unlocked door wide and charged into a man who was carrying a wicker basket of candy bars.

The basket went up and the candy bars went flying like schrapnel from a grenade. The man's feet were swept out from under him and he fell to the wood floor, hard, on his back. A throw rug sailed out the still open front door and the man gasped for breath as Harmon kneeled over him, one foot on either side of his torso.

"You giving out these candy bars?" he barked into the man's face, wrapping his fingers in the guy's sweatshirt. The guy he held was young, overweight, balding. He was sweating because the house was too warm. His eyes were close-set.

"Wha... wha..." the guy said.

"These Mars Bars!" Harmon barked, grabbing for one of them. He tore it open, finding another two pins inside. "These don't come like this from the store!" he yelled, crushing the candy in his fist and punching the guy in the face with it. "These don't come with bones!" He punched the guy in the face again.

He grabbed the guy's sweatshirt in both hands and dragged him to his feet. He turned him around and slammed him face first into the stairway bannister that hugged the left wall. Then he glanced back, kicking the front door closed with his foot.

The front door didn't close immediately, but Scott Harmon didn't know that. Daremo slipped inside and then shut it silently behind him. By then Harmon was dragging the sweatshirted guy into the living room. He dragged him across the carpet and threw him onto the couch. He jumped on him and hit him in the kidney. He turned the guy over and hit him in the stomach. He pushed his head back so that it smacked into the wall.

"Where'd you get these?" Harmon demanded, one knee on the couch, his right fist cocked.

"Hey, man, hey man," the man mumbled through bloody lips. Harmon hit him again, across the jaw. It almost had the same effect as a slap, only more painful. The guy's head snapped to the right and then back, as if his neck were an industrial-strength rubber band. The fog faded from his eyes.

"Where?" Scott demanded.

"At the store!" the beaten guy exclaimed defensively.

"Oh yeah?" Scott growled, throwing the mushed candy bar in his fist into the guy's face. He smeared the crushed chocolate from his palms across the guy's puss by slapping him repeatedly. Scott grabbed him by the neck. "The store, huh?" He dragged him off the couch and into the foyer again. He threw him against the bannister. The man's skull broke a bannister support before he fell face first onto the hardwood floor.

Scott grabbed an uncrushed bar and unwrapped it as the guy slowly got to his feet. Scott spun him around, grabbed him by the throat, and pushed the candy bar up to his lips.

"From the store, huh? So nothing's wrong with them, then. So eat it, buddy. Come on, eat it!" The man tried to turn his head away. He wriggled in Scott's grip. "Come on, eat it!"

"I don't want to!" the man screeched, trying to fight back. Scott pushed the bar into the guy's face until the pin inside pricked his palm. He hardly felt it. The guy shrieked when the butt end of the pin touched his cheek. Scott threw down the squashed bar and started hitting the guy again—over and over, so the back of the guy's head bounced off the bannister. Then he threw the guy into the opposite wall. When the guy slid down to the floor, Harmon kicked him in the balls and then in the side until he broke a few of the guy's ribs.

"Stop that! Stop that!" he heard someone shrieking behind him. He turned to see an old woman midway down the stairs, looking at him in shock.

"This your son, lady?"

The strength and conviction of Harmon's voice offered the woman little option but to answer. "Yes. What are you doing to him?"

"I'm beating the shit out of him, lady. You want to know why, just take a look at some of the candy he's been giving the neighborhood kids."

"What are you talking about?"

"He put pins in the candy bars, lady."

"That's impossible!"

Harmon could hear in the woman's voice that it wasn't. He could see in the way she looked down at her son that it wasn't. But he could see and hear all that as his own mouth continued working.

"I don't have to search his room, lady. I know what I'd find. Rubber cement and a box of pins."

"Who are you?"

Harmon looked down at the cringing, nearly unconscious man at his feet, then walked toward the door. He only paused when he was outside. "I'm your neighbor, lady."

"Which one?" she called after him.

"All of them," he called back.

Nice touch, that. Daremo hung around until he saw that the woman wasn't about to follow in her son's footsteps. She was dealing with a problem child, and whatever she did to have caused it, she wasn't the kind who put pins in Halloween candy.

The young man would be in the hospital for a while. His mom called the ambulance and tidied up the dark apartment while she waited for them to arrive. The place wasn't cheesily decorated. It was just old. The father had died or taken off, and everything dated back to the heyday of the marriage. Like a lot of the elderly's apartments, the bulbs were dim and everything was as faded and yellowing as the people themselves.

Daremo surveyed the bloodied young man in the sweatshirt. He was a classic street bully, a cowed, pathetic young hood who only had brains enough to be afraid of everything. He wouldn't sue Harmon once he recovered. He would steer clear of him and not do anything out of line in the neighborhood again. He would probably even respect the man. If things had worked out, he might have even become Scott's friend.

Daremo left the way he had come—unseen, unheard, unfelt. He walked over to Mr. B's. It was the classic hole; a big, low, wide room with a bar all the way along the side wall, a small dance floor along the opposite wall, a bunch of tables between the dance floor, and a line of booths that were between the tables and the bar. Daremo knew what was noisier, the music or the conversation: the music, but just barely.

The place was especially loud that night. It was Halloween, and everybody wanted to have fun. A couple of people were in costume. There were pirates and hookers, but the best one was a huge Felix the Cat costume. Real cute. All the waitresses were dressed in dark brown plastic garbage bags that had been torn and taped in the shape of mini-dresses. They all wore heavy makeup in honor of All-Hallow's Eve.

Scott Harmon was at the bar. He had found a couple of his neighborhood friends there, as they almost always were on weekend or holiday nights. They worked in the Bridgeport factories nearby and knew of nothing else. They didn't have in-laws or families to be with. By the time Daremo reached them, they were already comfortably settled.

"I just hope it all . . ." Harmon was saying, his hand making a dying out motion. "There's always somebody . . ."

"He won't do it again," said the dark-haired man next to him with calm certainty, as if he would see to it. There was no doubting his voice and there was no doubting the face: Calm, wide-set eyes. Thin mouth. Dark skin. A nose mashed almost flat on the face with a deep, clean groove of a scar diagonally across it.

Daremo knew where he was now. He was sitting in at an unofficial meeting of the neighborhood grievance committee.

"It doesn't make any difference, Alan," Scott complained. "He's already done it. You read about this in the paper, and . . . you know, I used to think it couldn't happen here. I knew we were in for trouble when I realized it could happen here. Right here. Down the street. So I hoped it wouldn't happen. I hoped it would just keep away from here for a while longer. Until I was gone, maybe.

"Somehow I knew, though. Somehow I knew that this was the year. Today was the day. . . . Man, I hope Halloween just dies out, that trick-and-treating just stops. It isn't worth it, man."

"Hell, the kids like it, Scott," said a heavier set guy next to Alan.

"It isn't worth it, Phil," he maintained. "Even without this shit, it's just more sugar for the kids. It just rots their teeth and makes them fat."

"Hey, Scott," Phil said jokingly, "you going to wipe out Christmas next?"

"It's not the same thing," Harmon countered, ignoring the humorous tone. "At Christmas, the parents have some control. They can give the kids some nice stuff. But not at Halloween. All they get is candy."

"Hey, there's a lot of sugar and sweet stuff during the holidays too, Scott." Phil ignored his own previous joking tone. Scott was discussing the situation and he wasn't about to just cave in and agree. This is what they did when they weren't making a living. They talked just like this. "All those pies and stuff at Thanksgiving. And, man, you know there's all sorts of candy at Christmas."

"Come on, Phil, it's not the same! There's some control at Christmas and Thanksgiving. You know what your kids are getting."

"But there's a lot of sweets, still. A lot of candy."

"Yeah, I know, but *you're* giving them the stuff. Not some strangers."

"Yeah . . ." Phil reluctantly agreed, leaving the word open for any argument he could come up with. When he couldn't come up with anything, he busied himself with trying to catch the bartender's eye for another round. On him.

Another neighbor, Jim, sitting to Scott's left, took up the slack. "Hey, shouldn't we be telling all the others? The neighbors, I mean. Probably a lot of the other kids got those candy bars too."

"I went up to every house on the block," Scott said. "I left notes for anybody who wasn't home."

"What did you write?" Phil wanted to know.

"I just told them that the Mars Bars might have some pins in them and that they shouldn't be eaten." Harmon was interrupted by a guy bumping into him and sloshing his beer on the bar top. The bumper's own beer went onto Alan. The dark-haired, wiry man was instantly off the bar stool, his arms up. "Hey, hey, hey, watch it, will ya?"

The bumper spun toward Alan, his face fixed in an angry expression. He was a big guy with a wide head and a flushed face. He had a couple of inches on Alan and at least thirty-five pounds. He put a beefy hand on Alan's chest and pushed. "Watch where *you're* going!" The guy was drunk.

"Hey, you bumped into me," Alan said evenly, not backing down.

"The hell I did, asshole," the man slurred.

"Mister," Scott said to him, "I was sitting right here

the whole time and you just dumped your beer on him."

"Keep out of this, motherfucker," the man shouted into Harmon's face. "What are you doing, cocksucker, ganging up on me?" He raised a hand to push the seated man, but Harmon grabbed his wrist and twisted. Suddenly the bumper was on bended knee before the bar.

"You like this hand?" Scott inquired mildly. "Take a walk."

The bartender was signaling the bouncer. Scott saw it. He let go of the guy's wrist and sat back. The guy went immediately to his feet, unsteadily. He had to step back. Frank the bouncer was beside him just as he began to move forward again.

"Everything all right here?" he asked.

"Just fine," Scott assured him. "This guy's just had a little too much to drink and spilled some beer on my friend."

Frank knew his job. He looked over everyone involved quickly. "Hey, maybe you've had a little too much, buddy," he said, the threat clear in his otherwise reasonable voice.

"Hey, I'm okay," the bumper said quickly but without hostility. "I didn't mean it." He searched out Alan with unfocused eyes. "Let me buy you a drink." He slapped a dollar down on the bar.

"Thanks," Alan said, taking the bill. "But I'll use it for laundry expenses."

"Come on, pal," Frank said, taking the bumper's arm. "You've had enough." He carefully guided the complaining man to the front door. Phil and Jim smiled at the two others, visibly relaxing.

"Nicely done," Phil said.

"Too bad," said Scott. "I felt like taking the guy apart." Alan resumed his seat, taking his damp shirt front between two fingers and fluttering it.

"Too bad," he said. "Now the thing's going to stink like Stroh's."

"Al," Phil laughed. "All your shirts stink like Stroh's!"

"Schlitz," Al corrected. "Bud, maybe. But never Stroh's, Jack."

The two others laughed. But not Scott. "I don't know," he said quietly. "I don't know if it's worth it anymore." He turned to look at Alan, who returned his gaze evenly. "I kept at it because, you know, if I didn't, who would? You get behind your country, your hometown, because it's, like, where you live, you know? I mean, I've got to live here, you've got to live here. We can't go around stinking up the street and then expect everybody else not to."

The others just listened and tried not to look directly at him. They weren't thinkers. They didn't have the machinery to tell him that he was getting older, his wife was pregnant, he was saddled with a decent job he couldn't afford to leave, and the serpent was right around the corner.

They didn't know the serpent. They didn't think about having to look in the serpent's eye one day and ask, Is this it? I mean, Is this what my whole life adds up to? A job, a wife, some kids, a mortgage? I mean, is that *it*? Is *that* why I was born?

So they just stared at him, not really thinking about what he was saying or what it meant to him. Or even what it meant to them.

"Damnit, I'm getting tired of this," Harmon groaned, rubbing his eyes. "Nobody's playing back-up. Everybody's just trying to tear everything down." That was as far as Harmon could go as well. He couldn't put it in any better words. Daremo let new words spiral in his own mind.

They don't know what they're doing. They're tearing down their own houses, their own streets, their own cities, their own states, their own nation. And they're acting as if it won't all come back to them, as if they can still laugh when everything is torn down. But they won't laugh. They won't party.

Daremo grinned. No wonder no one talked like that. No wonder these men didn't put such feelings into words. When they were put into words, they sounded really stupid.

"It's the night," Alan told Harmon. "It's just the fucking night, Scott. Let's go home."

They said their goodbyes to the others and made their way toward the door. The bumper was waiting for them outside.

"I want my buck back," he told Alan.

Harmon looked around. It wasn't that late, but it was late enough. Late enough on a holiday. Late enough on a school night. Late enough to have the sky studded with stars, late enough to have the streets fairly empty of cars and completely empty of people, and late enough to have the parking lot almost deserted.

"Take it easy," Scott started.

"Keep out of this, asshole," the guy snarled. "This is between me and your friend here."

Harmon sighed. "You've called me a motherfucker, a cocksucker, and an asshole, buddy. I think that makes it between you and me. Don't you, Sinatra?"

The bumper ignored him, trusting in the basic law of the streets. Two regular, nice guys wouldn't gang up on him. "I want my buck back."

Scott looked at Alan. Alan looked at Scott. Alan looked at the bumper. The bumper looked upset.

"All right," Alan agreed. "All right. If you're that intent on fighting, then we'll fight." Alan's tone was temperate, resigned.

"But you've been around," he continued, looking up at the man. "You know the way these things work. You'll get a couple of shots in, I'll get a couple of shots in." That sounded just fine to the bumper. He got set. His shoulders hunched down and his fists came up.

Then Alan's tone changed. "But I'll tell you," he said quietly, evenly. "No matter what happens, I'll be going for your eyes. And sooner or later, I'll get them."

The bumper straightened up, blinking. He stared into Alan's face. He saw the serpent. He heard his mama calling. But he couldn't back down. His expression began to cave in. He had lost the edge. Hell, the edge was on another planet by now.

"You want your dollar back?" Alan asked him reasonably. The bumper nodded. Alan took it out of his pocket, ripped it into sixteen pieces, and let all of them flutter to the ground. "You got it. See you around."

Alan and Scott walked away. The bumper stared at the shredded bill, then went quietly to his car.

Daremo showed himself in Scott Harmon's backyard. It was a little after eleven-thirty, time for the working man to be in bed. Scott had little knowledge of the world after eleven on week nights. Come to think of it, even on weekends. He had to be at work at eight in the morning. But tonight was a bit different. Tonight, the cruel world had caught up to his house.

Everybody in the house—the renters on the first floor, his brother-in-law on the second, and his wife on the third—was in bed. Only he stayed up, sipping a beer in the lawn chair on the driveway in the backyard. The lawn chair was the metal and plastic fold-out kind, getting worn at the seat. The driveway came from the street along the right side of the house and swung to the left before the three-car barn/garage. The yard was pretty large for Stratford, stretching almost thirty yards from the back door.

"Who are you?" Harmon asked as the Ninja Master appeared from the shadows, almost right in front of him. Normally, Harmon would have started at the sudden appearance, but Daremo allowed himself to seemingly take shape before Scott's eyes—slowly, unthreateningly.

"Moe," he said.

"Like the Three Stooges?"

Daremo thought of Hama and Archer. "Similar," he nodded.

"What do you want? Just passing through? There's a

fence behind the garage, so you can't get through there. And there's a doberman next door. I wouldn't walk through that yard if I were you."

Daremo shook his head. "Just wanted to talk. That was a good thing you did tonight."

"You live around here?"

Daremo could see in his face that Scott wouldn't believe him even if he said yes. Scott *knew* his neighborhood. When Scott was certain of something, even if he was wrong, he was certain. The good thing about Scott, though, was that if you proved him wrong, he'd back down. Some folks wouldn't. But in this case, he was dead on the money.

Daremo shook his head. "Mind if I sit down?"

"Go ahead." Harmon motioned toward another chair, folded and leaning against the garage. "Want a beer?"

"No thanks," Daremo said, getting the seat. "Just a talk."

Harmon shrugged, looking back toward the house: the hundred and twenty-six-thousand-dollar house. The house he had to help pay off. The house with the balloon mortgage and the pregnant wife in the plain bed upstairs. "What about?"

"About Scott Harmon," Daremo said, sitting a few feet away from him. "Vietnam vet, second louie Red Beret. Thirty-five years old, almost thirty-six, getting tired, getting worried."

Harmon's eyes narrowed. "You told me your first name. Now who the hell are you?"

"Watch close," Daremo suggested. He looked around. There was a big maple tree next to the garage, over his shoulder. He put the walking stick across his knees. He pulled the *ninja-to* blade from inside of it very slowly and very carefully.

"She-it." Harmon breathed in awe at the splendor of the sword. He had a fleeting thought of it stuck in his chest or slitting his throat, but Daremo's manner belied the fears. The stranger with the sword pointed at a dying leaf hanging away from the others just over the edge of the garage wall. Harmon nodded to acknowledge he saw it.

Daremo carefully laid the *ninja-to* across his lap, then pulled the *wakizashi* blade from the other part of the stick and threw it, fast. The short blade went right through the leaf's stem, a full thirty feet away, even though Daremo threw the spear as if tossing away a cigarette.

Scott looked back at the stranger, impressed, but Moe was pointing back toward the garage. Scott turned to see the leaf falling toward the driveway. Daremo threw the *ninja-to* like a Frisbee. It spun through the air like a horizontal buzzsaw. It flew so fast Scott could hardly see it.

When he could see it clearly again, it was sticking in the tree trunk. The falling leaf was pinioned in the bark by the blade.

Harmon didn't look back at the stranger for several seconds. He wanted to make sure he wasn't drunk or seeing things. He waited until Daremo ran toward the tree and leaped into it. Daremo jumped almost ten feet in the air, grabbing the branch the leaf had been cut from and pulling himself up in one smooth motion. The branch hardly shook.

Almost immediately, Moe was on the ground again, the *wakizashi* spear in his hand. He pulled the *ninja-to* blade from the tree trunk, cleaned the blades on his pants leg, and slid them back in place.

"Can I see that?" Harmon asked quietly when Moe walked back. Daremo handed him the forty-six-inch-tall walking stick as he returned to sit down.

It was nearly seamless. Even though Scott knew there were two blades in it, he couldn't clearly pick out the breaks in the seemingly solid piece of wood. It was an incredible piece of work.

"Where did you get this?"

"I made it."

Scott twisted one end and started pulling out the *ninja-to*.

"Don't run your thumb along the edge," Moe suggested. He didn't have to continue. The blade almost frightened the ex-soldier. He instinctively knew it could cut right through any finger as if going through marzipan.

"Where did you get these?"

Daremo told him.

Scott stared at him, slack-jawed. "Who the hell *are* you?" Harmon asked for a third time.

Daremo told him that, too. Everything.

3

Crystal-clear blue skies with white wisps of clouds. Clean warm air caressing chestnut-brown soil. There is a God, and He, She, or It made all this.

Just look at Africa. It has an astonishing geological structure, with an amazing temperature range. It has forests, grasslands, papyrus swamps, and deserts, grows livestock, millet, corn, coffee, peanuts, cocoa, rubber, fruit, wheat, and rice, and yields coal, petroleum, natural gas, radium, iron, cobalt, chromium, uranium, and gold, gold, gold.

Just take a plane. Shoot down across the western Sahara and over Mali and Niger, and land in Nigeria. Take a tinier plane from there, sail around Chad, and you can drop into the accurately named Central African Empire, also known as the Central African Republic.

Land in the capital, Banqui, and take a car southwest

into the montane grassland. You're on the Equator, so it's hot all the time. But it's a crisp kind of hot—not like the jolly jungle land of Southeast Asia. But you're on the African latitude of the equivalent tropical rain forest. Close, but no cigar.

Mike Barnes wouldn't get anywhere closer to it. Not after his experiences in 'Nam.

Harmon and Daremo got out of the Land Rover as the dull orange metal albatross roared ten thousand feet along the horizon.

"There she is," Scott said proudly, smiling with his teeth. The big airplane was reflected in both his mirrored sunglass lenses.

"Pretty," Moe said, watching the hulking aircraft maneuver like a Cessna two-seater. It was the airplane version of an overweight middle-aged man trying to prove that he was still macho. And he wasn't doing a half bad job of it, either. But the plane would have to land before Daremo could see how bad the hunk would feel in the morning.

It looked like the Ninja Master didn't have long to wait. "She's coming in," Harmon said. The men looked around, guessing what would serve as the runway. There was some flattened grassland between baobab trees on either side of their car. Harmon stood close to the vehicle as Daremo studied the plane's approach carefully.

Mike was going to show off. He was bringing his winged baby down into a tight stretch of yellowing ground to their right. The space between trees was just enough for the wingspan. Both men watched, Daremo the far more impassive, as Barnes belly-flopped the craft on three wheels.

"Come on," Harmon called over the rumble of the plane. "Let's meet him." They both swung into the Rover and drove toward the slowing aircraft.

STREET LETHAL was stenciled on the big nose, the small black letters almost lost on the C1-30's girth. The gold dust of the makeshift runway shrouded the words in sunshine-fog as the pilot threw open the side door and leaned out.

"Hey, Louie!" he shouted at Harmon as the driver strode toward the still-humming plane.

"Hey, Knight!" Scott called back. "Get down here."

Barnes didn't stand on ceremony. He jumped out of the plane, hit the ground, rolled, and came up on his feet. He walked right into Harmon and the two started hugging.

"Who's this?" the pilot asked, still holding Harmon with one arm. Scott made Moe's intro, but Barnes introduced himself. "Mike Barnes, knight errant and black as night. At your service, man." He and Daremo did a combination handshake and high-five.

He wasn't black as night. Nowhere close, but to anyone south of here, he would do. The white South Africans thought of anything darker than milk as pitch black. Barnes was shorter than the two others, about five-eight, but he was solidly built, with strong cheekbones, dark eyes, short kinked black hair, and a wide, thick nose.

"Yeah, maybe," Daremo said, looking at *Street Lethal* more than Mike Barnes. "Let's take her up."

Barnes brought Harmon up to date in the sky. "I'm a black rubber ball, baby," he said. "I bounce from Nigeria to Zaire, from Angola to Zambia, from Zimbabwe to Mozambique, from Tanzania to Uganda. Wherever the money is decent."

"You ship anything?" Harmon asked from the co-pilot's seat in the cramped cockpit.

"Anything. These are all my brothers down here, man. Ain't no side better than the other. But what I really like doing is side trips to Namibia. Anything to help get them from under Southie's thumb."

"Good luck," said Daremo. The United Nations had declared Southwest Africa free and named it Namibia, but the white South African government declared the move illegal. It wanted to keep all the black boys down on every farm it could.

"Thanks," Barnes said, glancing back at the third passenger, in the navigator's foldout seat. "Am I going to need it?"

Daremo considered it. The Herc flew well, and Barnes knew what he was doing behind the wheel. And he was another of Harmon's Heroes. They had everything else. What they really needed now was the C1-30 Hercules aircraft and the pilot.

"Yeah, you're going to need it," Daremo said. Barnes looked to his former commander.

"You're in," Scott said.

"In what?" Barnes asked. "What's the pot?"

Harmon looked at the Ninja Master for approval or suggestion.

Daremo stood up and went to check the hold's

condition. "An equal share," they both heard as he disappeared out of the cockpit.

"Of what?" Barnes asked.

Harmon smiled and clapped him on the shoulder. "You just won the lottery, old buddy. Maybe a million, maybe up to fifty million."

Barnes took his eyes off the sky. "Who do I have to kill?"

Twelve other guys now sat in the hold of the plane. Time had passed, more of Brett Wallace's money had been spent, and the team was outfitted—ready to go.

They had all taken vacations. They had all gone to various European tourist traps, then carefully made their way to Banqui. Barnes, Harmon, and Daremo were waiting for them there.

They took off at one in the morning, refueled in Ethiopia, right next to the Red Sea, and took off again fifteen minutes later. Barnes had to fly two hours sneaking up Saudi Arabia, skimming over Kuwait, speeding over the Persian Gulf, walking the tightrope line along the border of Kurdistan, then straight up the gut of the border between Iran and Iraq.

The craft was a speck in the vast night. It was going from one place to another, that's all. Nothing on the ground made any difference. The lines on the map were irrelevant.

The others left Barnes alone. All save Ken Murphy. He was the backup pilot, the ex-Ranger, the "mentor," as they called him. He had been in Vietnam in the good old, bad old days. He had been a ranger in jolly jungle land when they were still using leftover weapons from World War II and nobody was allowed a sidearm.

He told stories and argued with Harmon about nearly everything, but together they had hammered out a good plan. Scott knew when to back down. Murphy was the voice of experience. His hair had thinned and gotten slick, his gut and chin had grown, but he worked in international finance now. He knew where they were going.

He had been there before. He had seen it with his own eyes. He had the maps and he had the memory. He also had the doberman. He was Scott Harmon's next door neighbor.

Brett Wallace had found an ex-Green Beret in one house and an ex-Ranger in the next. One had contacts with a bunch of good old boys and the other had all the knowledge of their target. Wallace had hunted and picked until he found the nucleus for Daremo's future.

Ken knew the place, Scott knew the people. Ex-Rangers, ex-Green and Red Berets. All growing older, more dissatisfied. They weren't doing this out of greed; they were doing it out of desperation.

They were Daremo's children. They had been born of fire. They lived in the fire. When it died out, they grew weak. They redirected their energies to play *Obligation!* You know that game: it's bigger than Monopoly, bigger than Risk. You've played it. Or tried to. Go to school, get a clique, get a girlfriend, get a diploma, get a job, get a car, get a wife, get a kid, get a house, and keep going. Don't look, don't look! If you look, it won't make sense.

Harmon was a peeker. They were all peekers. They saw the cracks as they sped by. But what were they going to do? Do what they really wanted? Take a dream *seriously*? But *noooooo-body* does that! Get a girl get a job get a house.

They played along until Daremo arrived. Then everything fell into place. They could have their cake and eat it too. Get a wife, get a house, get a job, get a million dollars, get a kid.

Nobody was talking on this trip. The radio man, demolition man, and ten Rangers were checking their equipment—the best equipment Brett Wallace's money could buy.

They all wore basic khaki and camouflage shirts, pants, and jackets, with black storm-trooper boots. Their sidearms were army .45 caliber automatics, their business weapons, MP40's and M3's left over from the Second World War. Murphy knew where to get them. Harmon carried his favorite, a BAR—Browning Automatic Rifle with armor piercing shells. Schonberger had an Uzi—not surprisingly, since he had been an Israeli paratrooper at twenty-one. Palmer, the highest ranked master of Kokushiryu Goshinho Jujitsu, had an M16. Most of the others had AR15's, the international copy of the M16—which Barnes knew how to get hold of.

Daremo and Oshikata, the demolitions man, took care of the rest of the stock: a bag of grenades; two Claymores; two pounds C-4 explosive; two M-79 grenade launchers; two LAWS rockets/portable bazookas; two knapsacks full of fifty-caliber bullets.

The group's attention was diverted by a crackle coming over Richards's radio. It was the cockpit testing the connection and giving the signal. They had passed the Kuhha Ye Zagros mountain range. Ten minutes until Tehran.

In January 1979, Mohammed Reza Shah Pahlavi left Iran. On February 1, 1979, Ayatolla Ruhollah Khomeini, renowned scholar of Islamic law, returned from exile, and was greeted by three million people. And on April 1, 1979, the Ayatollah Khomeini declared Iran an Islamic republic.

In October 1979, Harmon's Heroes were on their way. T-minus ten minutes and counting.

The thirteen men in the Herc C1-30's cavernous cargo hold huddled together for a final briefing. Daremo led them through their paces verbally. They listened to Daremo, no matter how erratically the man appeared and disappeared. He had been there at their recruitment. He had the final word. Whenever he wasn't there, Lieutenant Harmon had the final say. Daremo hadn't been there for weeks before the word came through to take "vacations."

It made no difference by then. Each man knew his job. Each man pumped himself up like a member of a Super Bowl team. Some prayed. Everybody got ready to go.

Oshikata strapped on his pack of explosives. Alan Pierce, Harmon's best friend, took the LAWS. Schonberger took one grenade launcher, Bourgeau, the Colorado survivalist, the other. Aponte took one sack of the fifty-caliber rounds; Steve Ellroy, the ex-cop from Detroit, took the other. Bill Stone had the Claymores. Richards had the radio. Harmon secured his BAR. Daremo slipped his walking stick over his shoulder. The others hefted their rifles. They all wore the Ranger night parachutes.

"We're coming in at three hundred and fifty feet," they all heard Barnes say over the radio Richards held. His voice was unearthly in the otherwise silent hold.

"You've got ten minutes," Murphy said. "Fifteen tops. After that, even these idiots'll be able to get missiles after us."

Daremos scowled. The reminder was unnecessary. Only the countdown was necessary. Barnes started it. "Thirty seconds . . . twenty . . . fifteen . . . ten."

Richards took over. Schonberger opened and stood by the door, double-checking his "students"—he had supplied supplemental training for the group in the year that had passed since Daremo's first meeting with Harmon.

"One," Richards finally said, and the men dropped out of the plane like a string of pearls.

They fell through the night, feeling like gods. It was better than sex, because sex didn't have a tangible pot of gold at the end of the rainbow. An orgasm couldn't compare to this. They had a purpose, a goal, and a prize. No matter what happened, they would never be able to recreate this thrill, and would never want to.

The black parachutes opened. The men stayed in position, as difficult as that was for these semiretired soldiers. No one panicked; no one lost control. It was a testament to their abilities and to Daremo's judgment. He could pick 'em. Man, could he pick 'em.

They had some leeway north to south. They had almost no leeway in the other directions. They *had* to keep in a line. Each man maneuvered his sleek, rectangular Ranger parachute to stay next to his neighbor.

Harmon, Daremo, Palmer, Hale, Stone, Arocho, Aponte, Pierce, Oshikata, Ellroy, Bourgeau, Richards, and Schonberger landed like floating Rockettes in a ragged line along Tactjamischid Street. Tactjamischid, the "throne of the king." Only Richards fell to his knees. The others landed upright. Schonberger landed, and helped Richards up.

Every man instantly bunched up his parachute, cutting holes in the fabric with a pocket knife so the wind wouldn't carry it away. Within seconds, all the cloth was off and underfoot.

Oshikata and Stone ran to the west side of the street, heading toward a low marble-faced concrete building that looked like a horse stable. Aponte, Ellroy, Arocho, Hale, and Richards headed to the east, where there was a tall mud/brick wall. They crouched next to it. Without waiting for them to take their positions, Daremo led Harmon, Schonberger, Bourgeau, Pierce, and Palmer double-time down the street.

He took a right down a three-block alley that ran parallel to Eisenhower Street, the five others right behind him. He took a hard left when the alley emptied onto Roosevelt. At least those *were* the names of the streets. Who knew what Khomeini was naming them now.

It made no difference. Whatever it was called, the Central Bank—the Bank of Melli—was where Kenneth

Murphy had left it. Roosevelt Street was just another Iranian road. It was wide, it was plain, it was quiet, and it was clear. Nobody walked the streets with the Ayatollah calling the shots. Not at three o'clock in the morning.

Schonberger and Bourgeau ran to the front gate. Pierce raced around to the side wall. He handed a LAWS off to Harmon, who sped alongside. Palmer covered their backs. Daremo did a circuit around the entire bank, then joined Palmer. They crouched side by side, a few feet behind Scott and Alan, their AR15's at the ready.

Daremo whistled.

4

All hell broke loose.

Daremo cried out in fear.

The creatures raged into his vision, their animal faces on their sweaty human bodies contorted into expressions of hate, horror, and madness.

They swept at Daremo like gusts of wind. They screamed and shook their ancient, legendary weapons at him.

Ogres, oxen, horse heads, red-haired devils, trident-carrying demons—all taunted and terrified the dying man.

I'm going to hell! He cried out in a small boy's voice. The fiery pit—flame-filled, but black and bottomless at the same time—was under him.

I'm going to hell! He could hardly get the words out, he was crying so hard.

Daremo tried to make them go away, but he was too scared. He could see death coming. He could see it as something beyond blackness—a horrid emptiness. A terrible, terrible end from which there was no escape. Eternity was the most frightening thing of all.

He writhed, he shrieked, he tried to scramble away. His mind said the magic word. *Live*. He was going to live! He had to concentrate on the *other* images—not the demon faces: the others. The faces . . . of his friends.

Rick Aponte: wide skull, coarse skin, open, trusting . . . Stu Richards: round head, pale flesh, small, deep brown eyes . . . Alan Pierce: long face, dark darting eyes, thin tight lips, assured expression, knees bent, arms up, LAWS on his shoulder, FIRE!

Harmon blasted his rocket immediately after Pierce's. The detonations mingled. The side wall of the Central Bank erupted in flying concrete and twisted metal bars. The pair threw down the now useless mini-bazooka tubes and charged the cloud of brownish-white acrid smoke that rolled toward them like a fog bank. Daremo and Palmer moved behind them, backward, always watchful for anything that moved.

Schonberger and Bourgeau immediately launched the first mortar/grenade from the gate when they heard the explosion from the side of the bunkerlike building. Their explosives vaulted up in a lazy arc. The Israeli's grenade detonated as it dropped in front of the white wood and glass doors. It smashed the crystalline panes and tore out sections of cross hatching. The Cajun's grenade hit the steps and exploded on the first bounce, ripping out handfuls of the supports and chunks of the marble stairs.

The bank seemed to rock under the double assault. The four guards inside didn't have a chance. The pair at the door were knocked down by the blast from the side, then thrown forward when the entrance was assailed. They were just getting up when the two at the vault appeared in the foyer.

Schonberger and Bourgeau ran for the entrance, the Cajun shooting into the smoke as he went. They carried their rifles in one hand and the grenade launchers in the others. Bourgeau knelt beside the door as Schonberger threw himself into the opening. The guards inside were just deciding what to do when the Israeli opened up.

The Uzi could spit out more than five hundred rounds a minute. Schonberger didn't have five hundred bullets and didn't fire for a minute. The thirty-two-round clip was more than enough to perforate the stunned guards in five seconds flat. Schonberger buzzed some lead across the fallen guards' backs, then brought the close-range weapon to bear on the standing guards. One was twisted around before falling. The other had started running toward an alarm box near the vault when the lead caught up to him: one slug in the back of the leg, one in the kidney, one in the spine. The guard's hands spasmed up and he dove forward onto a desk.

Schonberger raced inside, checking the rest of the two-room bank as Bourgeau turned the grenade launchers around to face the street. As the Cajun started blasting apart the bank yard's outer wall, Schonberger considered the vault door. They had been wise to attack the side. The safe itself was one sweet motherfucker.

He ran to rejoin his partner as Willie Palmer jumped through the hole in the side of the bank and into the vault. He was there because he was small and fast. He could get through the hole easily, and while he didn't carry any extra ammo or explosives, he did carry canvas bags, which he started filling with jewels immediately.

The vault interior was unimpressive. The walls were reinforced concrete, and the shelving was simple wood. But on the shelves were diamonds and other gems, paper money, coins, and bars of gold. The gems were first priority. Palmer had four minutes to clean out as much of the store as possible.

Alan Pierce was soon inside with him, helping out. Pierce had a discerning eye. He went through the vault like a starving shopper on speed. There was only enough room for the two men to shovel comfortably. Daremo and Harmon made sure they had an exit when the time came. The ninja and the Green Beret louie crouched along the side wall, on either side of the smoking hole, waiting the probably interminable two hundred and forty seconds until the next phase kicked in.

No more than thirty seconds later, back down Tactjamischid Street, the stablelike building lit up like a long fluorescent lamp. Oshikata and Bill Stone were kneeling across the street at the base of the wall. Aponte, Richards, Hale, Ellroy, and Arocho were on the wall itself, lying across the top of it.

Ellroy glanced behind him. The Tehran airport lay stretched out in all directions. He could see the Phantoms and F-15s lined up to the left. To the right was just what the doctor had ordered: Jeeps, trucks, and the ever-wonderful, always beautiful APCs—Armored Personnel Carriers. Beyond this military parking lot was the public section of the airport: quiet, dimly lit, distant.

Ellroy looked back quickly when he heard the stable doors opening. Instead of horses, out came soldiers. It was the Tehran barracks, filled with the Ayatollah's best: on call twenty-four hours a day. Time's up, guys! The alarm is going off at the bank. They charged out the front door, still dressing, heading across the road to pile into the army vehicles.

Oshikata gripped the wires in his hands. He had attached them to a tiny box with a simple metal click-switch. The black-rubber-coated wires led from the box, across the road, to what looked like a pair of small audio speakers. Oshikata waited until Richards was ready to scream. To the radio man's eyes, the Iranian soldiers were spreading like oil—too much, too quick to contain. The Oriental *had* to be fucking up. This was it. The whole plan would fall apart!

Oshikata flicked the switch two seconds after Richards was sure the whole thing was over. The Claymores—the "speakers"—erupted.

The speakers leaped in place, barfing out a net of schrapnel. It was a giant dragnet of small silver balls, chunks of steel, and shards of metal. It fanned out, slicing everything in its path with a sizzling hum. The soldiers in front were cut down like harvested wheat. The ones behind reeled back as if battered by invisible fists or stung by killer bees. They stumbled, twisting in place, falling forward, falling back, knocked down by stinging pain that seemed to rip their skin from the inside.

"Go!" Oshikata hissed, chopping with one arm toward Aponte and Ellroy. The two tall men slipped down on the other side of the wall and raced toward the motor vehicles.

Stone and Oshikata opened up on the fallen and panicked soldiers with their AR15's. Richards fired from his position on the wall with his M3. Arocho and Hale surveyed the scene from the top of the wall for a moment before chasing after Aponte and Ellroy. When the first pair reached the APCs, the latter two had already climbed up to the twin turrets of the vehicle and were loading the bullet belts from their packs into the fifty-caliber machine guns mounted there.

"Should we take two?" Hale asked as Arocho climbed behind the wheel. He meant vehicles.

"We don't want to give them too many targets," Aponte growled. "We all get away together or we all die together."

Arocho twisted the engine ignition tab and pushed the start button. The APC, bought from America by the Shah, coughed, then roared to life. Hale jumped in as Arocho sent the vehicle lurching forward. Ellroy and Aponte grabbed the mounted guns to stay on top of the thing.

Arocho handled the APC as if it were a van on I-95. He sent it unerringly through the military entrance—simply a break in the airport wall midway between the vehicles and the jets—then took the hard left onto

Tactjamischid. As the thing lumbered down the road toward the other mercenaries, Aponte and Ellroy opened up on the barracks with the fifty cals.

Oshikata ran out to meet the thing on the road and leaped on, waving and screaming at the two on the turrets. "Stop! Cut it! We want them to go to the bank, not here!"

Aponte immediately let up on the trigger and waved at Ellroy to do the same. Nobody and nothing was moving inside the building or on the lawn.

"Believe me," Oshikata promised. "The Claymores would get anybody who was doing anything."

Most of his assurance was lost in the bellow of the APC's engine as Arocho gunned it toward Fardosi Square. Richards and Stone had already climbed aboard and were holding on for dear life. The lights on the Pahlavi Expressway twinkled in the distance as Arocho seemed intent on doing a wheelie around the weird monument at the square. Oshikata and the others saw the four sweeping sides of the sculpture fly by as Arocho got onto Eisenhower Avenue.

The wheels tore down that straightaway for three blocks. Arocho pulled the huge armory on wheels around on Roosevelt Street and drove through the ruined gate of the bank. He tore up the small lawn until the back of the vehicle was staring at the hole in the side wall.

Stone, Hale, and Oshikata leaped off and charged toward the safe opening. Schonberger and Bourgeau came around the corner and held tight there, still watching the street front. Daremo and Harmon raced around to cover the back. Aponte and Ellroy could cover the sides with the fifty calibers.

Oshikata dove through the hole in the wall. That was Palmer and Pierce's signal to start shoveling the bags out. They threw them, then Hale and Stone caught them and hurled them into the APC. Oshikata ran around the safe interior, slapping C-4 on the wall.

"That's it!" Richards bellowed. He was time spotter. Their four minutes were up. They had to get out of there—*now*. Palmer and Pierce threw two more bags and carried the last four out themselves, one in each hand. All four men climbed onto the vehicle. Daremo sent Harmon back to signal the front men. Schonberger and Bourgeau came when they were called. Daremo strode back to pull Oshikata through the hole in the wall.

Everybody grabbed on to the APC and Arocho charged the back wall. The vehicle smashed into the obstruction but, to everyone's horror, did not go through. It balked, then choked, then ground in place. Arocho instantly put it into reverse, saved the engine from blowing out, and went out the way he had come: backward.

"If this goes down the toilet," Hale yelled at him from the passenger seat, "you've got a calling in a New York cab!" Arocho grinned through the curtain of sweat shining his craterous face as he faced the APC forward on Roosevelt Street.

Both men's heads spun around when Oshikata detonated the C-4 inside the bank vault. That safe door *was* a piece of work, all right. It held. The back of the building collapsed. All that gold—those bars that were too heavy to transport—all the rare treasures that were too unwieldy to take out, were buried in rubble. The three walls around the safe became loose debris. There was now a bank facade and a pile of garbage.

Daremo climbed up between the turrets as the APC went from Roosevelt back to Eisenhower. "Police station coming up on your right!" he shouted to the fifty-cal men. "Nuke it." Harmon gave the others the same instructions.

The police station was like almost all the other buildings—bunkerlike concrete with marble fronting. They had just gotten the word when armored vehicle came thundering up. It was scurrying-ant time from Aponte and Ellroy's point of view. The machine guns backed in their hands as they lathered the building and parked police cars with the fifty-caliber mini-missiles.

It was as if somebody pulled a plug that deflated the entire area. The cars seemed to explode, the engine hoods leaping up, the windshields and windows shattering, the tires exploding. The bullets scraped along the marble and concrete walls, slicing out entire sections. Any person caught in the hail was torn apart as if by two giant hands and then thrown away.

Schonberger and Bourgeau chucked grenades one after another. Once the APC howled by, the bombs detonated, tearing holes in everything—flesh, stone, and metal. One grenade bounced under a police car, setting off a chain reaction of exploding vehicles. Daremo smiled. The attack could not have been better. Everyone who was *anyone* left in town would go racing for the bank and police station . . . not the airport.

"Now! Now!" Richards yelled into the radio.

"Nice signal," said Palmer.

"Subtle," said Pierce.

"I like that."

The men were beginning to banter, but not to loosen up. They were just expending a little tension. The most difficult part was still to come. The APC shot down the avenue, passing several fire trucks coming from the airport. Arocho aimed the heavy vehicle at the chain-link fence entrance to the public airway. Two more guards tried to wave them aside or slow them down, but had to get out of the way when the APC crashed through.

Daremo held on as the truck made a huge circuit of the grounds. Arocho pulled at the steering wheel until the carrier swept toward the parked jets. Schonberger and Bourgeau didn't stand on ceremony. They instinctively started chucking grenades at the planes. Aponte and Ellroy blasted at them with the hot 'n' heavy machine guns.

"Blow those fuckers!" Hale cried, emptying his own weapon into the planes as they passed.

Daremo and Harmon crouched side by side, aiming carefully—Harmon with the BAR, Daremo with an MP40. Each man blasted off a burst of rounds. Each man's target exploded They had hit the gas tanks on a pair of planes.

The APC rocked on its wheels as the shock wave pushed the men back. They all ducked as the debris came raining down on the tarmac. Arocho wrenched the steering wheel around, trying to avoid the smoking chunks of F-15 that fell from overhead. A chunk of fusilage slammed into one turret, then bounced and slid to the ground.

Steve Ellroy was instantly up out of the unscathed turret, but Daremo was already waving him back, crawling toward the damaged machine gun post. He looked inside. Rick Aponte was lying on the ceiling floor, his eyes crossed, his arms moving feebly. The debris had bent in part of the turret—probably where Aponte's head had been. He was only stunned.

Daremo applied acupressure to his neck and shoulders, clearing away the fog. Aponte smiled when he looked up. Daremo looked up as well. They were pacing the Herc C1-30. It was coming in for a landing parallel to them. Things only stayed that way for a second. The huge plane's speed took effect and coursed ahead of the vehicle. Arocho pulled the APC closer to the runway, where Barnes and Murphy were bringing *Street Lethal* in.

Daremo looked behind. The carnage of the exploded jets was spreading to the other motionless fighter planes. He looked down to see Harmon taking in the same view. The louie looked up, and the men exchanged smiles. The year of training had not been in vain. The years of training for 'Nam before that were held in good stead. Hell, they were Americans. They were a bunch of yahoo Captain Americas. They could do anything.

The Herc touched down. Barnes slammed on the brakes. Murphy opened the back. Arocho drove hell for leather right at the lowering ramp. The C1 wasn't even stopping. It was just slowing down. The land vehicle had to get into the air vehicle before it turned around to take off down the same runway.

No problem. The ramp scraped up sparks from the asphalt as Arocho threaded the needle. He put the APC right in the belly of the whale. Most of the men bellowed in triumph and delight. Murphy immediately started pulling the ramp up. Daremo leaped off the vehicle, yelling for Schonberger and Bourgeau to follow him.

He ran for the rear of the plane as it made the turn at the end of the runway. He grabbed the men's grenade launchers as Barnes poured on the steam in the opposite direction, preparing for takeoff. Daremo scrambled up the rising ramp, holding a grenade launcher in each hand. He fired them at the same time.

Harmon joined the Israeli and Cajun—all three men's mouths slack—as Daremo slid back down the now closed ramp with the grenade launchers still in his hands. The louie stared at him in wonder. No broken wrists? No broken wrists. The man had put a pothole in the runway the size of a Volkswagen. If any Phantom could still be made airworthy, it would have to take off cockeyed.

The takeoff threw everybody to the floor. The plane seemed to rip into the sky. Barnes was giving his winged baby all the juice he and it had. But within seconds, everybody could move again. As soon as they could stand, they started celebrating. The quartet walked back to the main body of the group, accompanied by their cheers. Almost everyone was shouting; they were clapping each other on the back, shoulders, hands, and butts.

"Anybody got any champagne?" Richards yelled. Almost all of them laughed at that. Only Daremo didn't join in with the jubilation, and his was the most powerful personality. The others almost immediately quieted, each head soon turning toward him.

"We got six minutes," he said. "The airport is at ten thousand feet. The crest of Mount Darmavon is at sixteen thousand feet. We get over it in six minutes, then drop under radar range and hug the mountain range until we're out of the country. But they've got six minutes to get missiles after us. If they can."

"And if they get missiles after us," Harmon said gravely, "that's it."

The men looked at each other. The hold was silent for twelve seconds. "So now what do we do?" Bill Stone asked.

Harmon smiled. "I say we look at what we're willing to die for."

Everyone looked at Daremo. Pregnant, breathless pause. He grinned and nodded. Everybody relaxed. Some laughed. They all went to the APC to bathe in the booty.

"We did it."

The six minutes were up. Barnes had done a sickening drop on the other side of the mountain.

"We didn't do it yet."

Diamonds, pearls, rubies by the case. Gold and silver coins by the sackful.

"Any estimates?" Palmer inquired.

"I wouldn't hazard a guess," said Aponte.

"I would," said Stone. "Plenty." Most of them laughed in appreciation.

"What do you think, Moe?" Ellroy asked the Ninja Master. All eyes turned to him.

"Enough," said Daremo.

"Whatever happens from here on in," Harmon reminded them, "don't forget what we did. We got in. We got out. No casualties."

"None of ours, at any rate," Pierce said softly.

"Don't I get a purple heart?" Rick Aponte asked, pointing to the bandage on his forehead. More laughter.

"You get a Swiss bank account if it all works out," Harmon said. "But we're only halfway there yet."

"Strict adherence to the plan is absolutely imperative from now on," Daremo said. That calmed everyone down somewhat.

"We did it before," said Hale. "We'll do it again."

"This time, you're not in control," Daremo reminded him. "This time you have to hold it in, not shoot it out."

"Translation," said Harmon. "No going crazy. No getting drunk, no bragging, no bullshit."

"That's a capital offense," Schonberger said quietly.

The louie nodded. Daremo could see the understanding on their faces. They knew that all the gems were worthless if they didn't stay in control. They had to forget the possible wealth and concentrate on the joy of the battle. They had gotten a free vacation doing what they did best. They had had the time of their lives. Any subsequent reward had to be a pleasant fringe benefit.

They all started at a long drawn-out howl from the cockpit. "We're out of fuckin' Iran!" Mike Barnes hooted. The group went wild. They cheered to *Street Lethal*'s rafters. Ken Murphy came bustling into the hold.

"We've razzed the U.S.S.R.," he told them. "It's just a few klicks in that direction." He pointed west. "No," he corrected himself, pointing northeast. "That direction. Welcome to Turkey. Drive safely."

Barnes chose that moment to take the Herc into a big dip. Everybody's stomach went into their throats. The pilot slid the C1-30 down a Turkish mountainside as Daremo went over to Richards's radio. He set the dials and spoke a few words in Turkish.

Harmon looked at everyone and everyone looked back. It seemed Daremo had done a lot of field work when he wasn't at the Connecticut "training camp." They thought he had found a Turkish rebel leader who spoke English. It turned out they were right, but that didn't keep the ninja from learning Turkish himself. Just another language added to his list of world tongues.

Daremo went to the cockpit. After looking over Barnes's shoulder for several minutes, he spotted the lamplit makeshift runway. The pilot looked to the ninja for confirmation.

"I have a dream," Barnes said. "They lure us onto a fake runway. We crash. They sift through the rubble for the jewels."

"You're the man for this job, all right," Daremo told him.

"Black marketeers are all the same," Barnes said,
looking out through the windshield. "Makes no difference if they're in deepest, darkest Africa or the wilds of
Turkey."

"They don't know what we're carrying, and they can't
risk a fire. We've promised them all sorts of weapons.
They can't afford it all going up in smoke."

Barnes nodded first, then *Street Lethal* nodded, heading down for the lights. It turned out that the lamps
were torches stuck in the ground and the runway was a
patch of flat grassland in the hills around Silifke, on the
Mediterranean Sea. The Hercules aircraft landed perfectly on the short runway. Barnes's showing off in his
home base was no fluke. The C1-30 was well known for
its short takeoff and landing area, and Mike Barnes was
just the pilot to exploit that.

As the rear ramp slowly lowered, the Turkish mountain rebels slowly gathered, their Russian Siminov and
Mosin-Nagant rifles held at the ready. They raised the
torches they had pulled from the ground as the ramp
hit the dirt.

Their leader, a dirty, smelly, short, gnarly guy miss-
ing a front tooth, took the point, a nine-millimeter
Stechkin automatic pistol in his right hand and a Turkish
nine-millimeter MKE pistol in his left. Twenty-one
Turks stood outside the plane. Fourteen Americans
came down the ramp—backlit by the naked lightbulbs
inside the Herc's hold.

"Throw down your weapons!" the Turkish rebel leader called out in English. "As a sign of faith."

"Why not?" said Scott Harmon casually, dropping his

BAR. "They're yours anyway." To the Turks' surprise, all the other Americans threw down their rifles without so much as a stiffening of the shoulders or a discouraging word.

The leader's head moved back and his hairy chin jutted in, but he was not taken by surprise for long. "Your sidearms too," he called, sounding like he had found the catch.

Harmon folded his arms and shook his head. "That's not part of the deal. Remember? We give you rifles, ammunition, an Armored Personnel Carrier, and you let us walk out of here."

The Turkish chieftain ruminated on these facts for a few moments, then strode forward. He peered at Harmon carefully. His men raised their rifles accordingly. The Turks knew the Americans couldn't very well use a public landing strip.

"Wait!" the chief said suddenly. "I didn't make the deal with you!" he said gruffly, acting as if that negated the arrangement and he could do whatever he liked. "Where is the man I talked to?"

"I am that man," Harmon said. "So if you'll excuse us, we'll be going now. We have a boat to catch."

"No!" the chief boomed. "No, you are not the man! I am certain. You cannot go." He made a sudden motion with his hand. All the Turks aimed their rifles. Everyone beside Harmon tensed. When faced with gun barrels, their first instinct was to fight back.

"Steady," Harmon whispered warningly. Then the louie looked back at the chief, appearing chagrined, only slightly irritated. "That's not the deal, sir," he said affably.

"What do I care for your deals?" the Turk gloated. "You give me a radio to listen to every night for your signal. You pay me to make torchlit runway. You promise me guns. You have plenty of money to throw around. But now you are in my country, on my land. Why shouldn't I have everything?"

Harmon held up a single finger—the middle one of his left hand. "For one reason." He didn't elaborate.

"What reason?" Now the Turk was on the defensive.

"Because you're a magician." The chief stared at the louie as if he were nuts. "You can do a magic trick."

"What are you saying?"

"Watch. Go ahead. Point to any one of your men. Any one."

"You are insane, American." Still, the Turk couldn't bring himself to give the order to fire. Not when there were so many of them and all still had their army .45 automatics.

"Go ahead, point. Anybody. Or are you frightened?" The chief scoffed. "Crazy Yankee."

"Either you do it or I will."

The chief turned to his men. "Hey, we do magic tricks now!" he guffawed in Turkish. "He wants me to point at one of you. Hey, Malatya! How about you?"

It was a big game now. Malatya seemed pleased, lowering his gun and slapping himself on the chest.

"Point," Harmon suggested, motioning.

"All right, American!" the chief said. He pointed. Malatya dropped dead.

The stunned Turks hesitated. When their eyes returned to the Americans, all the .45's were out and aimed. "I have the power now," Harmon told the chief quickly, without a hint of humor. "Throw down your weapons." The louie only gave them a second. As soon as the chief did nothing, Harmon pointed at another Turk. He dropped dead.

"Throw down your weapons!" Harmon shouted in Turkish, a nifty phrase he had learned from Daremo. The rebels dropped their guns like bad borscht. Harmon shot their leader in the head. The other thirteen men opened fire on the remaining eighteen Turks.

In just a matter of seconds all the Turks lay on the ground. Harmon stood next to the men on the gangplank, looking down sadly at the carnage. As they watched, Daremo appeared from the left side. His *wakizashi* was unsheathed. He was holding it pointed at the ground, which made him look like a military park garbage collector. But instead of picking up refuse with the stick, Daremo stabbed each of the Turks to make sure none still lived.

He stood among the corpses, his expressionless face looking like a skull in the eerie lights of the torches. "Each of you find a body that's about your size," he told the men. "Put your uniform on him. Put him in the plane."

Barnes groaned. He could guess what was coming. "I'll bury the others," Daremo said quietly. He retrieved the black *shurikens* from the corpses while the strangely sedate mercenaries picked among the bodies for lookalikes.

Daremo sat hunched over in the cockpit of *Street Lethal*. He had his head in his hands. The dead sat in the hold, their mouths and eyes open for the most part.

The plane rumbled over the Mediterranean Sea, heading southwest.

Daremo dropped his hands to his lap. He stared straight ahead as the plane flew on. He had spoken at length with Schonberger. He had attached the remainder of Oshikata's C-4 to the floor of the aircraft, near the fuel tank. He had led the men to the Mediterranean and the boat that was waiting for them before returning to the Herc.

The men had liked the ship—a real tramp steamer, the kind Humphrey Bogart always booked passage on. The captain was a friend of the Israeli's from his merchant marine days. Now the man spent all his time ferrying folk along the scenic ports of Europe. He had his retainer and his instructions. It would be a lovely trip. Stops at Cyprus, Crete, Sicily, Corsica, Marseilles, Barcelona, Gibraltar, Algiers, Casablanca, and Lisbon.

The men would leave the ship at different ports, dropping their .45's onto the Mediterranean, Ionian, and Tyrrhenian seas as they disembarked. In Marseilles, Richard Aponte and Stuart Richards would take the duffel bags through France and into Switzerland. They had strict instructions about who to see at the French-Swiss border. Daremo had spent most of the remainder of Brett Wallace's money greasing those wheels.

In Zurich, the two money men were pretty much on

their own. They would have to investigate the various amoral and illegal brokers to get the best exchange rate for the hot goods while the others finished their "vacations" and went home. It would probably take months, maybe years. They might get as little as a dime on the dollar. But it was still a fortune split fifteen ways.

Yeah, Daremo knew how to pick 'em all right. Everybody would do okay; nobody would go off the deep end. Aponte and Richards had the know-how and adaptability to work together, creating a corporation that would pay the shareholders handsomely every year—and once things got rolling and the investments were made, even twice a year. And everybody would get his own personal Swiss bank account.

Daremo took the final Ranger chute and walked to the cargo door. It would be a beautiful explosion. Somebody somewhere was sure to see it. The authorities would investigate and find just enough to deduce that the daring band of bank robbers' luck had run out, that once they had made their successful getaway from Iran, the split had turned sour. For whatever reason, the aircraft, with all aboard, had crashed at sea. There were no survivors . . . and no hint as to the airplane's or mercenaries' identity.

Daremo turned around from the open door. His army of the dead stood among the group of Turkish dead—all the people he had killed who were with him all the time now. The three motorcycle hoods who had mutilated his family and who he had executed were way in the back. The Turks he had killed were standing at the front of the crowd, beside their own corpses. That's the way it worked: each new victim took his place at the head of the class.

They had all found places in the Herc's hold and now stared at Daremo, smiling.

Down and down and down Daremo fell. The army of the dead fell out of the plane behind him like a chuteless invasion force. It was the biggest airdrop no one had never seen.

A ball of fire. It was a big yellow tennis ball in the sky, all puffy and fuzzy as it rolled. Then pieces of the plane flew in every direction. The crash into the Mediterranean didn't make one big splash. It made eighty-three little splashes.

On November 4, 1979, less than a week after Harmon's Heroes' raid, Iranian militants took control of the American embassy in Tehran.

The CIA tried to get a line on the Melli bank robbers, but their concerns turned to the embassy problem when they didn't have the resources under the Carter administration to investigate the robbery properly. Officially, on the books, in the closed files, the robbers had died in a plane crash and the riches were at the bottom of the Mediterranean Sea.

Just how crippled the intelligence agency had become was obvious from the impotent American military attempt to rescue the hostages in April 1980. In July, the exiled Shah died. In September, an Iran/Iraq war broke out. The Ayatollah could certainly have used the money then. But he had never had the resources to find it.

Diversified investments.

Money market funds.

Holding companies.

Accruing interest.

Tax shelters.

There's a tiny office in the Empire State Building in New York City. On the sixth floor is a smoked glass door with the legend inscribed in black-outlined beige letters: Y.M.I. INCORPORATED. Once a year, thirteen men show up there for a board meeting and dinner. At the dinner, they always make the same toast:

"To magic."

Part Two

Armament is an important factor in war,
But not the decisive factor....
Man, not material, forms the decisive factor.

> Mao Tse-tung (1938)

There is still one absolute weapon....
That weapon is man himself.

> Matthew Ridgway (1953)

5

The Mediterranean dissolved. In its place came Hong Kong. The man stepped out the front doors of Kai Tak Airport. The winds from the harbor blew across the airport peninsula, cooling the commonplace Oriental humidity.

Who was he? He couldn't remember. He could see a face in his mind, but he couldn't attach a name to it. He could see moving pictures of the recent past.

He could see a man with hair and eyes the color of sand sitting in the darkness. He could see the man in bed with a red-haired, blue-eyed woman. He saw the man leave the bed and go through narrow, winding cobblestone streets to a small shop. He could see the name of the store as if through eyes smeared with Vaseline: the Afuia Bazaar.

Dark shapes. Voices. Veiled threats. To his astonishment, he saw the man cut down the moving dark shapes. The dark shapes were men. The man was slicing them with a sword.

Explosion. A hand made of shock and fire that hurled him through the back door and into a wall.

He felt the concussion in his gut. But he also felt the cunning. He felt the amazing mind working. He could see, he could smell, he could hear, he could feel through the senses of that man. But he also felt an astonishing array of new senses—senses he could not identify or name.

The man blocked a weapon, a hurled object he instantly identified as a *shuriken*, a ninja throwing star. He looked up to see his enemy: the Figure in Black. More taunts, more threats, and then back to the beautiful blue-eyed woman in the warm bed. Her eyes were closed; how did he know her eyes were blue? What was this ache in his heart?

He immediately scoffed at the sentiment. Heartache, indeed. But he couldn't deny feeling it. He couldn't get rid of it. He saw this woman walking beside him in the desert. He saw them walking until a hole appeared in the sand. He fell in, she didn't.

He saw her with another man—a one-armed man bleeding black blood. He felt something else then. The heartache graduated to excruciating, torturing pain, a pain that went beyond pain the way love went beyond pleasure, a pain he could barely control. He ran from it. The farther away he ran from the red-haired woman and the one-armed man, the better he felt.

The anguish of his recent adventure had forced him

to reorganize his mind. He must have used the plane flight to redesign his brain's workings. Naturally, he'd be a little disoriented when it was finished. Refreshed, he walked to the curb, certain in the knowledge that it would all come back to him. There was no reason he shouldn't nudge it along, however.

How did he get here? He did not know. It was as if waking from a living dream. The red-haired woman and one-armed man had been insubstantial, part of something that could have been a dream or a nightmare. But Hong Kong was real enough. The shrieks of Cantonese were all around him, as were the noxious fumes from the taxis and buses.

Strangely, the sights and sounds were not foreign to him. He understood the words. He wasn't intrigued by the seemingly new location. It appeared he was well versed in the area. His mind began shoveling information to his consciousness.

Why was he here? To see the Figure in Black. Why that? More mental images: the strange gunlike weapon in a dark-skinned man's hand, a weapon that numbed the brain. Another device: a box with two wires. The wires connect to the back of the head. A single red pencil-point of light. A brick wall in the brain. Mind-control devices.

The Figure in Black was the key to the mind-control devices. The devices had to be destroyed.

He felt better. Now he knew he was Daremo and he was in Hong Kong to find the Figure in Black, who would lead him to the inventor of these mind-control devices.

He stopped feeling better.

Illogical. One man? More like a team of Chinese scientists slaving for years.

No. One man.

He felt better again. It was only logical that the discoveries were too futuristically individualistic to be the work of a committee. Maybe a team took the finding of this brilliant person and realized them, but the advances that led to the weapons were the work of one man. They had to be. His mind told him they were.

He felt much better. He had it over most of the world's population. He knew who he was, where he was, and what his purpose was. He stamped down on the instep of the man behind him and swung the back of his right forearm into the man's face.

He was astonished by his actions and the reaction. The man's arms shot up and the man dove backward as if propelled by a circus cannon. He collided with a dolly-truck full of plastic and leather luggage a redcap was pulling toward a bus stop. The man went through the Samsonite wall and collapsed head first on the pavement. He somersaulted backward, his limbs lax, and flopped onto the sidewalk.

Nobody, including Daremo, was sure what had happened. The passersby whined and complained in shock. All they knew was that a man had flown backward, knocking over suitcases and causing some minor inconvenience and delays. Daremo looked down at his forearm in surprise. *Gooood* punch. He did an instant replay in his mind.

He had felt a displacement behind him: of energy, of air. He had seen a glint in his peripheral vision.

The skinny Chinese in the sunglasses and suit had come up behind Daremo, trying to stick a knife in his back, through his kidneys, or between his ribs. Instinctively, Daremo had stopped the action with a blindingly painful slam to the attacker's foot and then catapulted him back with a devastating forearm to the nose.

Daremo strode quickly to the taxi stand and slipped into a red car with a silver top. The driver immediately started chattering at him. *"Eeen chow laow cha quoin wah!"* He heard the sounds first, then the English words, as if he was getting a simultaneous translation.

"Hey, mister, you have to wait in line. I can't take you. You have to wait in line."

"We'll wait in line," Daremo told him flatly. "Start the meter running. We'll wait in line until it's your turn."

The man wasn't about to turn down extra money, so he shrugged and started the meter. He turned back and waited while the three cabs ahead of him got fares. Daremo sat back and took stock. He was wearing black shoes, comfortable dark-colored lightweight denims, and a black rugby shirt with a light brown collar. He had money—Hong Kong dollars—in his pocket. And that's all.

"Where to, mister?"

Daremo looked up, trying to dispell his confusion.

"Tsimshatsui," he said, the word coming into his brain as if rising from the bottom of a swimming pool.

It was their turn at the head of the line. As soon as

the car in front of him pulled out, Daremo's driver pulled out as well, leaving a cursing redcap in its carbon monoxide wake.

"Anywhere in particular in Tsimshatsui?" the cab driver asked as another ninety cents clicked onto the flagfall fee of HK $4.50. Daremo wasn't unduly concerned since it took almost seven Hong Kong dollars to make one U.S. bill.

"Laichikok Amusement Park."

"Laichikok? That's not exactly Tsimshatsui."

"Close enough."

The cabbie considered it. "Okay," he said, checking his watch.

There wasn't much to see outside this time of night. Daremo leaned back, trusting the driver not to gouge him. These HK hacks were strictly licensed, so it wasn't common practice. Besides, he had other things on his mind.

Daremo tried straightening up his mental desk. He concentrated. He saw an image of himself walking through customs. No luggage. Well, they couldn't very well detain him for that.

"I trust you'll have something for us to check coming back?"

"I expect so." Smile.

"How long will you be staying?"

"Not long."

"Two weeks?"

"At the most."

"Business or pleasure?"

"Very good, sir. Have a pleasant stay."

Daremo saw himself drop something in the garbage can as he left the airport. Back up the film. Freeze frame. Closeup. It was small, thin, and blue. It was a passport. Probably counterfeit. How else could he have gotten in?

Well, one mystery was cleared up. Now there was the question of the assassin. He had used a stiletto. Maybe the redcap had found it when cleaning up the fallen luggage. Maybe not. Maybe the assassin was dead. Maybe not. In any case, any investigation would not lead to him. No one but the assassin knew his target and he wasn't going to talk, alive or otherwise.

Moshuh Nanren? On an airport sidewalk with a shiv? Why not? It might have been the best way to surprise him. It was certainly the last thing he was expecting.

Of course, it was also the worst way to kill him. They couldn't figure that he'd be so intent on defending himself against possible superweapons that he'd miss the old switchblade up the caboose. A warning? The *Moshuh Nanren* didn't give out warnings! Or maybe they did. There was no way to tell with them. There was plot within subterfuge within doublecross.

Don't question; accept. There is no win or lose. Face it, fight it, go on. That was his motto. It was nice not caring. He could die any time. It made no difference to him if he saved the world or not. It made no difference to him if he defeated the *Moshuh Nanren* or didn't. The battle was the only thing that mattered. Life at the moment. If he won, he'd go on. If he didn't, it wouldn't make any difference to him. He'd be dead.

The highway was a mass of twisting roadways and

tiny, chattering cars. They took Princess Margaret Road to Hong Chong, a right on Gascoigne, past the Jordan MTR (Mass Transit Railway) station, along Jordan Road, a left onto Canton Road, and then a right onto Austin.

Daremo paid the driver and got out at the entrance to the park. Little children in Donald Duck, Star Wars, and Shoalin Temple T-shirts were going inside, accompanied by older men in loose short-sleeved white shirts, baggy beige pants, and puffy, padded coolie jackets. There were women as well, some wearing dresses, but most wearing the same outfits as the men.

There were some younger couples too, most of whom were dressed conservatively. Only one or two had on anything remotely considered Western hip. Daremo joined the crowd, getting little notice from the populace, who were used to tourist round-eyes. He paid his HK $3 to get in. The first thing he heard was a grinding hum. He looked up to see a mini-monorail scooting by, weaving in and out of the pine, banyan, and casuarina trees. There was also the refreshing tang of eucalyptus in the air.

The next thing he heard was the familiar, comforting sounds of pinball machines. Almost right next to the entrance was a penny arcade. The machines looked like they had been taken right out of Daremo's childhood haunts. They were certainly old enough to be the machines from Daremo's haunts.

He fought the urge to join the players and walked on through the neighboring small, sloping zoo, enjoying the sights of the various farm animals. There were chickens, pigs, buffalo, deer, and mucho monkeys. His eyes kept trying to seek out any tigers, but none were to be seen. What a gyp.

He continued on over the lovely crowded bridge. Below was a nicely tended manmade lake, around which countless Chinese lovers spooned. He passed an area of benches lined with food stands. He passed the side-by-side double cinemas. One was playing *Endangered Species*, starring Robert Uhrich and Jobeth Williams. The other was showing *Snake in the Eagle's Shadow*, starring Cheng Lung and Simon Yuen. They both looked pretty good.

Daremo didn't have time to see either the American or Hong Kong feature. His destination was just ahead. He heard the music first, or what went for music. To his Western ears, it sounded like a kind of fire alarm.

The amphitheater was simple enough. There were two sections of chairs with an aisle down the middle. Three-quarters of the seats—the ones closest to the stage—were filled. The back played host to a shifting sea of innocent bystanders. People would saunter by, stay for a while, and move on. Daremo did the same.

He watched for a few minutes as a beautiful woman, in a flowing white and blue gown, danced alongside an old man. The man had a long white beard, moustache, and mane. They seemed to flow with each other, standing side by side, the woman slightly in front. The old man was dressed in dark brown, with a white apron. He carried a short oar. To Daremo's delight, their subtle movements of mime and dance created the unmistakable feeling that both were in a boat on a river.

He smiled, looking around to share his feelings—his

appreciation of the Peking Opera performers' talent—
with those around him. He saw their smiling faces
directed at the stage. And he saw the Figure in Black
standing by a pine tree.

Daremo's expression froze. Was it possible that only
he could see the man? He was standing right next to
the tree, just to the left of the folding chairs. He was
dressed all in black, a black hood covering his head and
black visors covering his eyes.

He disappeared as Daremo watched him. He seemed
to meld with the tree. Daremo stood up and slowly
went to the pine. He saw the Figure moving away from
him, blending in and out of the night as he walked
deeper into the wood border of the park. He didn't race
from tree to tree, actively seeking to meld with darkness. He just walked fluidly forward. The darkness
seemed both to make way and course around him as he
moved—like he was walking through mist.

Daremo trotted after him. They kept this up until the
Figure reached the deepest section of the wood. Daremo
could still hear the Peking Opera performance and the
pinball machines in the distance, but all he could see
were tree trunks and the black outline of the Figure.

"We meet again." It was all he could think to say.

Bam! The first blow went right to his mind. It felt
like his forehead was a closet door and the Figure in
Black had kicked it open. Now all the junk he had been
shoving inside all these years was spilling out. He
grabbed on to a tree with his left arm to keep from
falling.

Daremo tried to slam the door shut. The Figure in

Black kicked it open again. Now he'd really done it. The Figure in Black had invited all his friends. Hundreds, literally hundreds, of human-shaped creatures came pouring into his mind.

"Hey," he called out to one.

A man with a club turned around. "Who, me?"

"Yeah, you. Who the heck are you?"

"I'm Favorable-Wind Ears."

"What are you doing here?"

"You're new in town. I heard you were having a party. I hear everything," he boasted proudly.

Daremo looked at all the other folk lounging around. They were beautifully dressed Orientals in ornate, detailed costumes. "Who are the rest of these . . ."

"Gods," said Favorable-Wind Ears.

"Gods?"

"Yeah, we're all gods. Hong Kong has a million of 'em. There are gods for houses, gods for streets, gods for vehicles, gods for everything. That's Tsai Shin, the shopkeeper god over there. There's Wan-Chung, the scholar's god. Look. Over here's Thousand-Mile Eyes. He can see everything . . ."

"That's enough," Daremo said in exasperation. "What are you guys doing here?"

"It's a signal, stupid," said Favorable-Wind Ears. "We're a sign. I thought you'd pick up on that right away."

Daremo was stymied. He just looked at them, unable to think.

"Look," said Favorable-Wind Ears reasonably. "You go to El Salvador, you see Central American gods. You go to Israel, you see Middle Eastern gods. Well you're in Hong Kong now, fella." He looked Daremo up and down. "We heard about you," he said with a wink.

The ludicrousness of the whole kaboodle was about the only thing that wasn't lost on Daremo. He remembered and acknowledged his mental images from El Salvador and Israel, but those had been somber affairs steeped in the rituals and beliefs of the areas.

Well they may have been Hong Kong gods, but it was his mind. With a sudden surge of assurance, he swept them out of his consciousness. The Laichikok Amusement Park returned and he still stood and he still lived—much to his surprise. The Figure in Black was right where he had been before. Daremo realized that less than a second had passed. He had blanked out within the parameters of a moment.

Yes, the Figure in Black said into his mind. He was answering Daremo's earlier greeting. He was also showing off his own psychic power.

Daremo remembered their previous confrontations. The fight in the Central American terrorist training camp. The fight in the Negev Desert. Their most recent meeting, the second-long exchange in the Israeli nuclear missile silo. Through these fleeting battles, Daremo had gained a limited understanding of his foe. And the one thing he knew for certain was that the Figure in Black, godlike, enjoyed taunts.

Daremo tried to play on that. "You called?"

That was all the Figure needed. Throughout their conflict, the man had alternated direct, deadly assaults with what could be laughingly termed playful, testing attacks—perhaps to see how proficient Daremo was. They were almost dress rehearsals for subsequent fights, dress rehearsals wherein the Figure could gauge how much more would be needed to kill the Ninja Master later. But in the past Daremo had always been able to turn the Figure's tests back on the enemy, he seemed clearly aware of.

Yes. We've fought . . . on your home ground . . . Now mine.

Daremo accepted the words, choosing to send none back, verbally or mentally.

You must fight to heart of Moshuh Nanren . . . yuàn yean jing.

"Is that an order?" The Figure had called him a round-eye. That deserved a snotty response.

I know who you want.

Not what, mind you, but who. Daremo was on the right track. The Figure wanted to goad him on, lead him into this trap. Daremo was more than happy to follow. Okay, *baka,* spring your damn traps. Come on, spring 'em!

You won't reach him.

The blade went right at his head. It was a short Japanese blade, no longer than eight inches. But it was two inches wide and wickedly pointed, with a plain light wood handle.

It was a *tanto,* the samurai dagger, used to behead the enemy. The Figure was doing his damnedest to make sure it served its traditional purpose, but the months between their confrontations had not slowed Daremo. His head moved. The blade went by his neck and stuck into the tree behind him. It sank five inches into the bark meat.

Daremo was already rolling to his left side, desperately trying to keep his hands from reaching for the *shurikens* he knew were not there. He hadn't risked secreting any in his belt (or anyplace else) for fear of discovery by airport customs.

When he had reached his feet, the Figure was directly in front of him, Wing Chun.

Wing Chun—"hope for the future," the martial art developed over two hundred years to be one of the most efficient. It was the form of short blows and sudden, explosive kicks, perfect for in-fighting. The Figure's arms shot out like hydraulic pistons, trying to break through Daremo's preliminary defenses, trying to batter ribs, break septum, stop heart.

If someone were to discover them in the woods, it would look like the two were playing an elaborate signaling game. If seen from a distance, it would look like a dance.

The Figure attacked with Fok Sao the back of the palm, the wrist stabbing at Daremo's face.

Daremo countered with a Kan Sao block, and a Jut Sao arm-drop strike!

The Figure executed Cheun Sao, switch-arm block, strike!

Daremo threw a Pak Sao sweeping block, knocking the thrust away, with Bil Jee thrusting fingers at his opponent's shoulder.

Back with a Huen Sao rotating-hand block, Tan Sao, Tan Sao.

Kan Sao block, Gum Sao pin attempt.

Pak Sao slapping block, Bil Sao thrust, Po Pi Tserng! The Figure's hand struck Daremo under the sternum, then the double palm blow smashed into his chest, sending him back.

The ninja let the blow set his feet dancing, running backward, his arms windmilling to protect him from any sudden reattack. The Figure ran forward, after him. He dived forward and to the side, cartwheeling after Daremo, his feet together. He soared up, flying through the air in a side somersault, ready to attack again.

Daremo fell back, letting his backward momentum curl his body into a somersault, preparing to leap up toward the *tanto* stuck in the tree. Both men snapped out of their rolls, the Figure's leg karate kicking into Daremo's middle. The ninja's leap up the tree was cut abruptly, doubling him back like a folded arrow shot from the Figure's bow.

The ninja collapsed to the grass, lucky enough to have a downward incline below his shoulders. He used it as a base to vault backward from, trying to drag himself away from the Figure's attack. He threw himself backward to his feet, bringing his head up just as the Figure's foot slammed down where Daremo's head had been.

Daremo shot up, leaping in place in the air. The Figure shot his fingers toward the leaping man. Daremo grabbed the outstretched arm, pulling his torso away from the fingers and giving himself a vaulting-off point at the same time. Using the Figure's arm like a branch, Daremo threw himself over the Figure's head.

He somersaulted in a standing position over the Figure. The Figure kicked his right leg up. An incredible kick, straight up. The leg went out as if the Figure were kicking a football, but then it just kept going until the straight leg was bent all the way against the Figure's chest. His foot connected with Daremo's face as he was about to swing his legs to the ground.

Daremo was slammed around in midair. He spun in the wrong direction and landed on his feet, dazed, right next to the Figure. The Figure swung his elbow back. Daremo collapsed. The elbow hit a "rag doll," doing little damage. Daremo rolled like a barrel going downhill, away from the Figure's stamping foot. The Figure ran after him.

Daremo stopped suddenly, catching the stamping foot in both hands. He twisted. As the Figure spun away, he kicked Daremo in the side with his free foot. Daremo tried to ignore the pain as he vaulted to his feet, ran two steps, and leaped into the air—diving for the *tanto*.

The Figure somersaulted, landing on bended legs, and sprang back, trying to use his body as an arrow into Daremo's torso. Daremo soared up, letting his hands miss the *tanto* hilt, letting his feet hit it instead—using it as another vaulting point. He leaped higher into the tree. He grabbed a branch and scrambled up into the fuzzy pine needles.

When he planted his feet on two branches and stiffened his back on the trunk, he prepared for the Figure's next onslaught. But the Figure was gone. The wood below was now empty of human movement. Only the grass and trees blew in the slight wind. And, thank Favorable-Wind Ears, the only thing dead was the leaves.

Pretty pitiful, but the strategy had worked. The Figure would either have had to scramble up the tree after him, putting himself in a very unfavorable position, or he would have had to try attacking from the branches. And no matter if they were *Moshuh Nanren*, fighting while balancing on a pine tree branch was ridiculous.

Daremo stayed where he was for several minutes, listening. He didn't want to hop down, la-di-da, only to find the Figure waiting for him. He waited until he was as certain as he could be that the Figure was gone. Daremo dropped out of the tree, wrenching the *tanto* from the trunk as he dropped. He landed, the blade held in the defensive position, his body ready for anything.

But he was alone in the little wood. He silently cursed himself and the eerie fight. He quickly went to rejoin the populace in the main section of the park.

They had fought silently, with no Bruce Lee animal shrieks or Sonny Chiba mucous snorts. They had fought to test each other's skills, and Daremo had come up lacking. Badly lacking. The Figure had better be the *Moshuh Nanren*'s best man or the Ninja Master was in deep yogurt.

He had no taste for the continuing Peking Opera performance when he got back to the amphitheater. He had found some newspaper in a refuse container and now wrapped the naked *tanto* blade carefully before

putting the knife under his shirt. He retraced his steps
and went out of the park. He stood on Austin Street,
wondering what he should do now. Street vendors
called to him, but he ignored them. He tried to get
inside himself, to *feel* the Figure's presence. Nothing.

So he relaxed. His mind was still on the mend after
the post-Israeli tuneup and lube job, so he just let
thoughts filter in any way they cared to. He trusted his
brain. That faith was soon rewarded. Images of the Star
Ferry appeared. It was the most popular form of trans-
portation to Hong Kong Island from Kowloon.

He was on Kowloon peninsula now. To the north
were the "New Territories"—the buffer between British-
controlled Hong Kong and the People's Republic. To
the east and west were the more than two hundred
Hong Kong islands that were rarely considered part of
the deal. To the south, across Hong Kong Harbor, was
Victoria. That was the British name for the main Hong
Kong island, "the" Hong Kong, but even the Limeys
didn't call it that.

It was just Hong Kong, or Hong Kong Island, to
everyone—Daremo too. He walked to the corner and
took a left on Canton Road. He shunted off questions
like "Now what was that fight all about?" and other
sundry concerns to concentrate on the sights and sounds.
He knew his mind would keep him informed in this
relaxed state. It only seemed to freeze up when he gave
it the third degree.

Now this was more like it. Hong Kong—more correctly,
Kowloon, at night. And Tsimshatsui at that. He was on
the edge of the shopping center. Take any Manhattan

small business street, condense it, cram three more blocks next to it, then pile two more on top of that, and you've got a Tsimshatsui block. A tourist could stand on a Tsimshatsui corner all day just looking at each individual sign.

The place was a masterpiece—or a nightmare, depending upon one's point of view—of space utilization. The area was a giant jigsaw puzzle of stores locked into each other in the most outlandish shapes. There were more digital and electronic jimcracks in any one square foot than in any one square mile of any representative American city. It boggled the mind.

Thankfully, Daremo was on the western edge of the heavy-duty area. To his right as he walked south was Kowloon Way. It was still crowded, but not like the crush just a few steps to the left. He passed Ocean Center, crammed with luxurious shops for those disembarking from luxury liners. Next to that was the Hong Kong Hotel, where a person could sleep overnight for a mere three hundred Hong Kong bucks. Then there was the Star House, home of the Student Travel Bureau.

Finally, he came to the Star Ferry terminal. It was a dock jutting out into Hong Kong Harbor. In the water on either side, the walla-wallas were already beginning to gather. That meant it had to be near eleven-thirty P.M.—the last run of the ferry from Kowloon to Hong Kong and vice versa. The walla-wallas were small motorboats that took latecomers back and forth . . . for five times the ferry prize.

Since the ferry was HK fifty cents, the outlay wasn't bank-breaking. Still, it *was* close to last call, so the crowd by the pier was substantial enough. There was a coin-operated turnstile at the gateway assisted by a change machine right next to it. Beyond that was a nifty gate arrangement that held the crowd back while the ferry passengers got off.

The old, quaint two-tiered ferry was coming in as Daremo watched. It looked a lot like any other ferry boat—the kind that could be seen from Manhattan east. The ship would dock within minutes. Within seconds Daremo was part of the waiting crowd, eating from a paper sack. He had bought a light dinner from a nearby vendor. In Tsimshatsui, there was no such thing as a faraway vendor.

He bit into the *cha siu bau*—barbequed pork bun— with satisfaction. It looked like a simple dinner roll. But it was filled with a mixture of roasted pork and chopped onions. He finished that off as the crowd began to surge slightly. He took out the *kai bau tsai*—steamed chicken bun—next. It looked like a big puffy snowball. He smashed it into the face of the man behind him.

He pushed down the man's arm, the one with the newspaper in it. The small .22 automatic beneath the newspaper, in the guy's hand, fell to the wharf. It didn't need a silencer. Daremo's spleen was supposed to be the silencer.

The man jerked in Daremo's grip, trying to wrench himself away and retrieve the gun. Daremo did his Pele impersonation. He kicked the pistol so that it slid through the network of legs around them and dropped off the end of the wharf. Daremo was pleased. After his pathetic showing at the amusement park, he was glad he could have timed and placed his kick so well. No one around them knew what was happening.

The man gasped. Daremo had locked his thumb and hand in an excruciatingly painful jujitsu hold. Any slight movement either man made could snap some bones. The man hunched over. Daremo smiled. Like his predecessor, this assassin was wearing a suit and sunglasses. At night? Maybe that was how they could spot one another, Daremo considered.

The passengers on the incoming ferry had been let off. The gate was opened. The waiting passengers for the return trip surged forward. Daremo took his assassin by the hand and led him to the ferry.

Daremo took his new friend across the lower deck, to the stairs, and onto the upper deck. An old woman "tsked" as they went by. To her, and to everybody else on board, the two men were holding hands. Not only were they flagrant fairies, but an interracial couple to boot.

"Really," Daremo said flatly. "Some people can't live with change."

Daremo led his friend to a nearly unoccupied section at the rear and leaned the man on the guard rail. He twisted the man's hand just enough to bend his torso over the water.

"Well, you've graduated to guns," Daremo said quietly in Cantonese.

"Pardon?" the man gasped.

Daremo refused to continue along that line. Instead, he used the universal greeting. "Take me to your leader."

That the guy understood. "No," he said between clenched teeth.

Much to his surprise, Daremo let him go. He pulled his hand back. When the useless limb collapsed, he held it in his other hand. He looked at Daremo from under knitted brows. He couldn't get himself to stand up straight yet. His bent nerves wouldn't allow it.

Daremo knew any more public inducement would be useless. When the Chinese said no, they meant no. Most of them spent their lives finding ornate ways to answer in the negative without saying no, so when the two-letter word was finally uttered, it was final. Threats of pain and death were also useless. That's what assassins get if they do tell. Pain and death were what they wanted once caught.

Oh, all right already, Daremo told his subconscious. I know, I know. This guy *couldn't* be *Moshuh Nanren*. Neither could the twerp at the airport. It was almost impossible for a great actor to play a bad actor, and even those who could played a bad actor magnificently.

These guys weren't great actors, period. They were bad assassins. Not masterful *Moshuh Nanren* playing bad assassins—just plain bad killers, hired help. And not particularly high priced at that. Daremo looked the pathetic man over. Thin, straight, greasy hair. Tiny little slit eyes. Bad teeth. Facial discoloration. Spots.

The man began to relax under Daremo's scrutiny. To release some of his own frustration, Daremo poked him quickly in two pressure points with his index finger. The man doubled over, then straightened, his arms bent, his elbows in. He ended up in a position that was neither one or the other—like a man trying desperately not to pee in his pants.

Daremo looked to his left. An old lady was walking toward them, a white purse clutched in her pudgy little hand. Her expression said she meant business. Oh great, Daremo thought. A representative of the Kowloon League of Public Morality, no doubt, about to give a stern lecture on the sins of homosexuality.

The woman stopped five feet before the pair, pointed at Daremo with her purse, opened her mouth, and pulled the trigger of the automatic hidden in her handbag.

6

Daremo sat in the garish, red-lit bar, drinking a HK $25
Coca-Cola. The place stank of old socks, vinegar, and
baby powder. The old sock smell came from the cheap
Chinese cigarettes, the vinegar smell came from the
bad, watered-down booze, and the baby powder came
from baby powder. It was the main air freshener. It was
sprinkled in the bathrooms and upstairs, to cover the
odor of excrement and . . . upstair things.

This was Wanchai, Hong Kong Island's red-light district. The lights are more a shade of pink now, considering how the midtown high-rises of the powerful international financial center had crowded out a good deal of
massage parlors, topless bars, tattoo parlors, and old-
fashioned brothels.

But some were still there, tucked into one section of
Lockhart Street. What a fitting name. There were more

locked hearts here than broken lights on Broadway. There were not many broken hearts, but there were some broken teeth—courtesy of Daremo. He had been on the rampage ever since the Star Ferry.

You don't shoot a ninja with a 7.62 in a purse. Not today, at any rate. Daremo, as always, saw it coming milliseconds before it happened. Even in the early days of his training, he could recognize and categorize the facial and arm muscles utilized in gun firing. The gun went off, he went down, and his leg went out. That was followed by both her legs flying up and her head meeting the ferry deck.

The female assassin had timed her attack well. Just as the gun was going off, the ferry was preparing to cast off. The gate was shut, the gangway was raised, the ropes were untied and, more importantly, the on-board bells rung. The bells covered the noise of the pistol shot. It also covered the noise of the woman's fall. It didn't cover the sight, though.

It also didn't cover the sight of the young male assassin throwing himself overboard. Daremo scooped up the woman's purse and ran downstairs before the other upper-deck passengers tried to help the unconscious woman. As the ferry left the pier, Daremo took a step on the lower deck railing and leaped back onto the wharf.

It was a very impressive jump, but the male assassin didn't get to see it. He was trying to escape the ferry's wake and find a place to climb back onto Kowloon. While he was waiting, Daremo melded with the shadows and went through the woman's purse. He pocketed the small automatic—a "type-51" Chinese army pistol—and her money.

This was great. Less than two hours in Hong Kong and he already had a bankroll and weapons collection.

There was no identification in the purse, and no extra ammo, so he tossed the handbag into the harbor just as the other assassin appeared, dragging himself onto the wharf.

The young man went. Daremo followed. He followed him to the Tsimshatsui station of the Mass Transit Railway line. He followed him into the tunnel, past the ticket machines, through the turnstiles, and onto the sleek subway car.

The railway car went through a tunnel beneath Hong Kong Harbor; first stop, Admiralty Station. Daremo followed the young man off the train. There, the turnstile sucked back the plastic ticket that the Tsimshatsui turnstile had coughed out, and let the men through. Thankfully, they weren't the only two going through, so the assassin didn't notice Daremo tailing him. It was possible that the assassin wouldn't have noticed even if Daremo were directly behind him. Such was ninja talent.

Daremo followed the gunman east to Wanchai. He followed him through the twisting, narrow alleyways that passed for side streets in this second oldest profession section of Hong Kong Island. The sidewalks were no longer crowded with Vietnam vets looking for a little R'n R before the next firefight. The Yankee joes were gone with the divine wind, and the bar girls were left to fend with the locals.

Daremo followed the assassin to the door of the Tulips Bar. There, he wrapped his fingers around the man's windpipe, pushed him against the wall, and had a charming heart to heart.

"It's all over now, baby blue," he said quietly, almost lifting the man off the pavement with a single hand.

The assassin tried to speak, but the five fingers wouldn't let him. He only wanted to profess innocence anyway.

"You don't live here, yellow peril," Daremo continued, "You're not meeting a date and you're not relaxing after a hard day. Give me a name."

The man continued to choke in the negative.

"It's too late," Daremo maintained. "You've led me here already. The only thing that's keeping you alive is me. I want a name."

The assassin saw the light. He gave Daremo a name. Kao Fei. Daremo's left forefinger moved toward the man's temple. At the last moment, it veered off to the assassin's neck. The ninja lay the young man down on the sidewalk. To all eyes, he would look like a drunk. Daremo went into the bar wondering why he hadn't killed the kid.

The waitresses were all topless, and almost all of them had bad teeth. Daremo's entrance nearly started a martial arts contest among the ladies. Probably the ninja's most deadly adversary is a predatory female, because these girls spotted the good-looking American as soon as he walked in, ninja training or no.

To these women anything that was over five feet ten inches, under two hundred pounds, and didn't have a colostomy bag was good looking; but an American always meant money.

The fight was clearly joined. Only the strongest and best-looking survived the run for his table. A sweet-looking girl with a nice smile and a minor moustache was seated first, asking him to buy her a drink. His cola gave new meaning to the term *soft drink*. Her champagne gave new meaning to the word *carbonated*. It was lemon/lime soda in a wineglass with a price tag of HK $40.

"I like you," she said to him in carefully enunciated sing-song English. She pulled off the "l" in *like* extremely well.

"I like you too," he said to her. "Excuse me a moment." He started to stand.

"Oh where are you going, darling?" she inquired sweetly, practically getting him in a headlock. To her amazement, she found herself facing the opposite direction a moment later, her arms empty.

"The bartender forgot the little umbrella in my drink," he told her when she spun around. Daremo wandered over to the bar to find the brawny bartender, with a moustache covering a harelip, waiting for him. He just looked at the American with veiled, sleepy eyes.

"Hey, don't you have anything a little more . . . exotic?" Daremo inquired, motioning toward the pouting girls.

"These aren't exotic?" the bartender asked flatly.

"No offense," said the wisenheimer American, "but they're just like the girls next store. And down the street. And around the corner." As he mentioned each locale, he pulled out another sheaf of bills. The first had been the male assassin's. The second was the female assassin's. And the third was his.

The bartender leaned back and nodded. "You want to go upstairs?"

Daremo leaned back too, pulled a red HK $100 bill off the pile, and put it on the bar top. "I guess I do." You bet your sweet ass I do. The person he was looking for certainly didn't have his office down here.

The bartender took the money off the bar, never to be seen again. "Poor Yin Ying will be so disappointed," he said, motioning to the moustached girl with his head. Daremo put a blue fifty-dollar bill on the bar. The barkeep took that too. "You want to relax, maybe have a massage, stay overnight? Right upstairs, mister. Please. I will phone ahead."

"*Um goi*," said Daremo. Thank you. "Only the best, remember. I'm willing to pay for it."

"The best?"

"The best." Logic dictated that the office in question would be closest to the most exclusive parlor.

"That comes high."

"So do I." The retort didn't make much sense, but maybe it worked in translation. In any case, Daremo went through the beaded doorway in the back, up the red-lit staircase, and to a plain wood door with no knob. There was a buzz and the door clicked open inward. Two muscular Orientals were waiting for him. They blocked a short hallway with three doors on each wall and an exit door at the other end.

"Thousand dollar," said one.

"You're kidding," said Daremo.

"Thousand dollar, one hour," he continued.

"Ten thousand one night," said the other.

Hey, then this was a real bargain. Daremo forked the cash over. One man closed the door, the other led Daremo down the hall. To his irritation, they stopped at the middle door on the right wall.

"Hey," he said, shaking his head and pointing to the last door. The Oriental shook his head just as definitely.

"No, no. You go here."

"I said I wanted the best."

"This is the best. The best."

"I want to go in there," Daremo maintained, pointing at the end door.

"No girl, no girl there," said the Oriental. "Come, you go here. The best. I promise."

Daremo acted as if he were reluctantly backing down. "Well, for a thousand bucks, she'd better be."

The Oriental opened the door. Daremo stepped in. The room was pathetically simple. It was big enough, he supposed, but the ceiling was extremely low. There were two windows on the side wall, looking out onto the street, and another window on the front wall, looking out onto Marsh Road. All three had frilly red curtains. The bed was opposite the third window. It was a tarnished brass affair with a mattress that was beginning to sag. The bedclothes were black satin.

There was a bureau next to the third window and a padded, high-topped winged chair with a blue-dot design next to that. The room was empty. There was a door next to the bed. It opened onto a bathroom. Out of that came a woman—a five-foot six-inch woman. A blonde woman. The blonde, hazel-eyed woman. A blonde, hazel-eyed white women. She froze when she saw him.

"Holy shit," she said.

Michelle Bowers lay across the bed naked. She was an astonishingly handsome American girl. She was about twenty-five years old, with a dancer's body and a showgirl's breasts. Her skin and pubic hair were light tan. She treated Daremo the way any homesick, experienced prostitute would treat him. She enjoyed him. And if that didn't beat all, he enjoyed her too.

He had planned to put her to sleep with acupressure once he had lulled her into a false sense of security, but it didn't quite work out that way. Things started to get a little funny during foreplay. She hadn't had the luxury of foreplay for quite some time, since her clientele were well-heeled Oriental businessmen. She gave them what they paid for and shipped them out.

Daremo was different, if you'll excuse the understatement. She had been dressed in a white lace robe, and that stayed on while they kissed. She approached his lips like a starving woman would approach hot and sour soup—gingerly at first, and then with an increasingly ravenous, appreciative appetite.

At first, Daremo had been as clinical as she was. Then it was memory, not passion, that intruded. Images floated up to his consciousness. Memories of a strict, simple, low-ceilinged teak room with a single mat on the floor. He was naked in the dim light of a sole candle. Into the room came a woman in a ceremonial mask and a kimono.

She wore nothing under the kimono. He never knew what was under the highly glossed black and white ceramic mask.

Every night for the next month the woman in the mask picturing a smiling geisha taught him sexual technique. First the basics, then the variations, then the forms of sensual power.

When Daremo's concentration had returned to Hong Kong and Bowers's bed, the kisses touched something in him also, something lost. Not the memories of the ninjutsu school, but something he instinctively felt he dreaded to reclaim. He didn't know what it was, but it was still distant enough for him to enjoy her company and desire.

"Oh this is wonderful," she said throatily, slipping off the robe. She leaned him back and began to tend to both their needs. She serviced him as she would service any man who paid extra, but she also, for her sake, continued her starving woman's meal. She enjoyed his body, his muscles, his skin. She partook of him as much for her own satisfaction as his.

"That's nice," she said when finished. She was speaking for herself, not cueing him.

Daremo took her shoulders in his hands and pulled her down beside him. He started by caressing her neck—restraining himself from putting her to sleep then. Instead of closing off her brain's blood supply, he altered his fingers' rhythm and target. By the time he was kissing her breasts, she was floating on a sea of acupressured pleasure.

She groaned and slowly writhed as he prepared to

mount her. He lay her on her back and watched her
eyes opening and closing slowly. He lay atop her. He
slid off, pulling his shirt on. When he stood, he was
pulling his pants up.

"What the..." she said, sitting up. "Hey," she finished when he had pushed her down.

"Don't move," he said as the door swung open.

Eight men piled in, spreading across the room on the
other side of the bed. They all had weapons. Three—
including the upstairs doorman—had metal bars, two
had hatchets, one had a blackjack, and one had a knife,
and the bartender had a nightstick.

"Get the hell out of..." Michelle started, clutching
the sheets to her throat.

Daremo had a hand on her shoulder. "Don't move,"
he repeated carefully, his eyes on the men. "And keep
quiet."

The man with the knife took the lead. He came
slowly around the bed, waving the knife back and forth
like an experienced street fighter. Daremo played along,
moving back, allowing his expression to become more
and more frightened. Michelle considered doing something, but the situation and the tone of Daremo's
warnings held her in check.

The tension rose to an almost unbearable pitch, and
then the man swung the knife forward with a burst of
speed and breath. The blade came up toward Daremo's
stomach. But his movements were a blur of flesh. The
knife missed him and kept going. Daremo slammed the
bottom of the knifer's arm with the top of his own,
forcing the blade into the ceiling. Daremo then slid the

tanto blade from his waistband and rammed it through the fleshy part of the knifer's lower arm.

There was a scarlet explosion. Blood spurted out in all directions, staining the mattress and Michelle's face. She gasped and choked, screaming when she saw the knifer fall back and his forearm remain. His hand was still wrapped around the knife. The knife blade was stuck in the ceiling. The weapon and the quarter-arm made a macabre chandelier.

Daremo continued his pistonlike blow into the blackjacker's face. The punch, made all the more powerful by the *tanto* hilt in his fist, sent the man backward with a sickening smack. The blackjacker crashed onto the bureau top.

Daremo let the momentum of the thrust carry him forward. With his free arm—the one he had used to catapult the knifer's arm up—he grabbed the baseboard of the bed and vaulted around, kicking one barman and one hatchet man in one head and one stomach. The barman went down. The hatchet man sat in the chair, knocking it over backward.

Michelle felt like she was watching the Olympics of death. Daremo was bouncing around the room like a gymnast on his freestyle program. The kick continued with him literally flying through the air and landing on his feet near the front wall. Once his legs were down, one was up again, smashing the second hatchet man across the face and landing on the bartender's arm.

He knocked the nightstick down and rammed the *tanto* into the bartender's head. He pulled the dying bartender around and hurled him into the last barman.

When the last man had fallen, he pulled the automatic from his pocket and shot them at point-blank range. Michelle screamed for almost every bullet.

He shot the closest men in the head and the first few men he had knocked down in the chests as they tried to get up. He killed them all with one bullet to spare in the eight-round clip. He turned the gun toward Michelle. She stared at him over the barrel, her eyes wide.

"Take me with you," she begged.

"No," he said.

"Get me out of here," she pleaded. "Please."

"Forget it," he said, leaving the room.

He took a step into the hall, a step to the right, and kicked in the last door. A carbon copy of the room he had just left was revealed, only it was decorated as an office, not a bedroom. The bathroom door was open. Daremo hopped to it, already realizing what had happened. He could hear the street sounds more clearly and he could feel a draft on his skin.

Sure enough, the bathroom window was wide open and Kao Fei was nowhere in sight. Daremo stuck his head out the window. The street was full of Kao Feis. Every Oriental on the street was looking up at him. He ducked back inside and moved quickly down the hall, passing right by Michelle, who was standing in her doorway.

She ran after him, dragging the blood-soaked satin top sheet with her. "I can help. Just rescue me from this hole."

He stopped at the door. He stared at her. He thought: *so why not burst into the room with sub-machine guns*

*and make the mattress Swiss cheese? Why take chances
with a man you've been trying to kill all day? With a
man who has already taken out one man with a knife
and two people with guns? Why? There could only be
one reason. Because there was a woman in bed with
that man who you wanted in one piece.*

Michelle was quite a piece of work, all right. Even
with the colored blonde hair, she was a fine example of
the American dream sex machine. And because Kao Fei
wanted her unscathed, Daremo wasn't dodging bullets.

"Come on, then," Daremo said, suddenly kicking the
door open. She started at the violence and power of the
blow, which practically tore the obstruction off its hinges.
He jumped down the stairs and made it halfway through
the beaded curtain before he noticed the men streaming in the bar's front door.

He turned to see Michelle still at the top of the
stairs. "Not that way," she said. "Follow me."

She didn't give him a chance to answer, just ran down
the hall. When he reached the top of the stairs she was,
again, nowhere to be seen. A moment later she came
out of her room with blue flat-bottomed suede boots on
her feet, pulling a blue dress over her head. Its hem
settled a few inches over her knees. It had a high, wide
U-neck and a V-shaped back. She tightened a thin pink
belt around her waist, which was made more difficult
by the lace bra and panties in her hand.

"Nice going, Conan," she said, trying to top off her
ensemble. "We could have used that door." They could
both hear the men coming up the stairs.

Daremo leaned into the doorway and shot the first

man in the leg. He screamed and fell down, taking everybody behind him along.

"Nice outfit," Daremo said as he moved past Michelle to the exit door at the end of the hall.

"Not there," Michelle said, moving by him to the door opposite the office. She opened that and walked by the two Orientals in the bed. "Hiya, Suze," she said, going to the bureau. The man next to the hooker stared at the white woman as if she had stepped from a dream.

Daremo's arm shot past Suze's face and into the side of the man's head. He toppled off the bed onto the floor. As Daremo's arm snapped back, his fingers cut off Suze's brain blood. She slipped into sleep.

Michelle dragged the bureau aside as Daremo closed the door. "Was that really necessary?" she asked as she revealed the small trap door on the wall.

"Can't have them describing me," he said as she opened the obstruction and started climbing in.

"Easy," he heard her grunt as she pulled her hips through. "You're the guy with me."

He dove and slithered into the passage behind the walls. She was sitting, pulling the panties over her boots. "Sheesh, give a girl a second, will you?" she whispered.

Daremo knelt, reached back through the small square, hole, and pulled the bureau back into place. "There's your second," he said.

She frowned. "You pulled that bureau back in place like it was made of balsa wood. You lift weights or something?"

He didn't answer, just looked around. Michelle

shrugged, then awkwardly got the panties on, awkwardly rocked up to her knees and started pulling down the shoulders of her dress. Daremo took her arm and pulled her to her feet.

"The bra can wait," he said, walking by her. The passage was two feet wide but tall. Michelle stuck the bra into one of the two diagonally slit pockets in the front of the dress.

"Not that way," she said patiently, starting in the opposite direction.

"Yes," said Daremo. "This way."

He didn't wait for her. He climbed the slats in the wall until he had reached the building's ceiling. He found a weak spot and pushed his arm through a section of the wood-reinforced tarpaper roof. He made a hole as big as the trap door and climbed through. By then Michelle was standing beneath the opening. His torso appeared to her upside down, his right arm extended, his hand out.

She gave him her hand. He took it by the wrist. She wrapped her strong fingers around his wrist. "Hold on," he said softly. He lifted her through the hole as if she weighed twenty pounds.

"Whew," she said in surprise, her hands on his chest, leaning against him. "I *like* you."

He left her standing there. As he walked up the slight incline to the apex of the roof, she took in the surroundings. They were on a small, flat level between buildings. The wall of the place next door rose two more stories to her left, and there was an alley two stories down to her right. Beyond that was another four-story wall.

In front of her was another, wider, alley. There was another low two-story ceiling across it. Beyond were more low, flat ceilings. It was dark and smelly up here. The only light came from the streets and the other buildings.

"They're all over the street," Daremo said as he came back from looking over the front roof.

"I know what they look like," Michelle told him.

"I don't have to know what they look like," he answered, checking out the surroundings. "I can see what they act like."

"Wow," she said sardonically to the face that wasn't looking at her. "Mr. Wizard."

He looked back to her on that. "How far can you jump?"

"What?" The "why, you're just another dip" tone was coming into her voice.

"Fuck it," he said purposely. He wasn't about to let this girl take the "queen of the world" route with him. He took her hand and walked her forward to the edge of the building. "Keep loose and keep quiet."

"What?" she repeated, sarcastically incredulous. Then he threw her across the alleyway.

He had picked her up like they were doing a pas de deux in a ballet and hurled her, upright, across the alley. She landed on her feet, fell, and rolled—pretty professionally. She hadn't even had time to exclaim before he was standing beside her.

"What?" she said again. Only this time it was the

only thing she could think of saying. Smiling, he once more took her by the hand. Together they walked hand in hand down the Wanchai street across the rooftops. How romantic.

"Don't you want to know why I became a hooker?"

"No."

"Boy, you're pretty direct, aren't you?"

"What do you want me to say? 'Not particularly?' 'I don't think so?' "

"Hmmmm, maybe. Why don't you try it and find out?"

"Because if I try it, you'll tell me, and I don't care."

"Pooh," she pouted. "You're no fun."

She rolled over onto her back. She was naked again, only this time the bed was in the middle of an Excelsior hotel room. The satin sheets were of higher quality, the view of the Causeway Bay was breathtaking, the carpet was wall-to-wall plush, and the ceiling didn't have an arm hanging down from it.

"Neither are you," Daremo told her, turning from the window. "All you ever want to talk about is yourself." He sat on the edge of the bed. He was fully clothed.

"A fascinating subject," she professed grandly. "Want to hear how I became a hooker?"

Daremo didn't want to hear. He didn't even want to be there. After climbing down from the roof at the end of the block, they had made their way to the more prosperous factory and warehouse area to the northeast of Wanchai. From there, it was only a hop, skip, and jump to the prestigious Hong Kong World Trade Center and its luxury hotel. And the closer they got to that, the friskier Michelle became.

By the time they reached the hotel lobby, she was hanging on Daremo's arm, chattering away in his ear, rubbing her breasts on his shoulder and her thighs on his hip as she led him inside. He wasn't interested in paying the four hundred and twenty dollars for the double room, but she maintained it would be the last—the very last—place Kao Fei's men would come looking for them.

Daremo didn't mind the idea of Kao Fei's men looking for him. He wanted it, in fact. So Michelle coughed up half the room fare. She had ripped it off the bodies of the eight corpses in her room. The bartender and doormen alone had enough scratch to keep her in Excelsior room service for a week.

Once upstairs, she wasn't very interested in living up to her side of the bargain. He had rescued her, so now she was supposed to help him. First, he had to hear her *Reader's Digest* condensed version of her life story— how she had been "acting" in California when the Oriental interests had offered her a contract and big money to star in Hong Kong. How things had changed once she arrived. How she had become a virtual prisoner, tricking for peanuts.

Then he had to play a game of Trollop Pursuit, that game where everyone exists to serve a beautiful woman's needs. It was the golddigger's national sport, with its national anthem "Girls Just Want To Have Fun."

Daremo knew the game. "I don't want to hear why you became a prostitute," he said.

"Hooker, darling," she corrected, cavorting on the bed. "Go ahead, say it. It won't hurt you. Hooker."

Daremo quickly grabbed her by the neck. He cut off her words with his clamping fingers without cutting off her air. He pulled her prone body to him. He talked directly into her face without moving from his seat on the edge of the bed.

"Hooker," he said. "You happy? Now, listen carefully. I do not think that I hold power over you. So you can stop thinking that you are actually holding power over me. You can stop showing off. You *are* beautiful, but you are also a tease. I am not a teasee. I want to know who is trying to kill me and I want to know why."

He let her go. She scrambled away from him as if she had just discovered a horse's head in her bed. She crawled to the other end of the mattress and huddled against the padded headboard. She hugged her knees to her chest and looked at him with fear and anger. Then she started to cry.

"Damn you," she said accusingly. "Damnit," she said, looking away.

"I don't want to know why you became a hooker," he told her quietly. "*You* want to know why you became a hooker. You want to try the story out on me to see if I buy it. If enough johns buy it, maybe you'll buy it too."

He shook his head. "But you won't buy it, Michelle. Because johns are stupid and pathetic. You can't believe what they say. And if they buy your story—*anything* you say—that just shows how stupid they are."

Michelle cut off her crying. It hadn't been artificial, but she wasn't going to give him any satisfaction. "Fuck you," she said.

"You've already done that," Daremo reminded her with a smile. "If I knew that was going to make me a john, I would have killed you then."

His smile was effective. His words were reasonable. Her stubborn pride was filed away for use at a later date. She came out of her ball and slid over to him. She sat on her knees next to him, her arm around his shoulder. "You wouldn't have killed me," she said with friendly assurance. "I *can* help you."

He looked at her face and gave her a crooked "end of lovers' tiff" smile. He kissed her. Because she wanted him to. She was trying to live out a fantasy. To get what he wanted, Daremo played a part in that fantasy. But it was going to be a part he wrote for himself, not one she wrote for him. The one she would write would have him playing the part she thought men always wanted her to play. The sex object.

She would have kept rolling around the bed and hopping around the room naked until she heated him up to the boiling part. Then she'd come over all coy and profess that they were the best of friends. Daremo didn't have time for that. He hadn't boiled for decades. But he couldn't reach her on anything but her fantasy level.

He crawled onto the bed and took her in his arms. "Why did you become a hooker?" he asked, holding her across his lap.

She tapped his chest twice with her fist, then put

both her hands on his torso. "I don't know really," she mused in a faraway voice, looking at the ceiling. "It seemed the best thing to do at the time."

Uh-huh, Daremo thought. "Come on," he said, pulling her and himself toward the pillows. They lay on the bed, cuddling. Daremo could see her fantasies and her thoughts. She was fantasizing that she could trust him, that he was her daydream lover—the man who didn't exist, the one she spent all her free time with.

Her thoughts were rolling stream-of-consciousness memories of her youth. The good times. The single moments from inspiring autumns where she was alone and happy. When she wasn't trying to drive everybody crazy with her body and desires. She remembered the moments of that other love: love of parents, love of home, love of friends.

She was a prostitute, a great prostitute. So she was a great actress. And a great actress called up memories to find insights for her great performances. These memories were of warmth and happiness. That was the way she wanted to feel.

Daremo didn't go into her mind for this information; he was guessing. He had opened Rachel Assaf's mind. He had opened Jeff Archer's mind. He had learned that once the psychic door was opened or the psychic bridge between minds was built, there was no closing it from either side. The new subject was free to explore the new communication.

He couldn't afford to open up everyone he met, for whatever reason. And he wasn't about to introduce Favorable-Wind Ears and his crew to Michelle Bowers.

Rachal Assaf . . . the red-haired girl in the warm bed . . . in the desert. Daremo remembered Israel.

"Why does Kao Fei have a contract out on me?" he asked. Michelle's serene face filled his vision. Their noses practically touched.

"Drugs. It has to be drugs." He didn't say anything. "In addition to prostitution, Kao Fei controls the drug traffic in the area. They go together, don't they? Drugs and sex?"

"And gambling."

"Yeah, but the only time I've ever heard of him doing this kind of number involved drugs. He never gets this wild over the girls or numbers."

"Girls and numbers don't make the kind of money drugs do."

"Yes they do, but they don't make you crazy the same way girls and numbers do."

"I could compliment you here."

"You mean, 'depends on the girl?' "

"Yeah."

"Why, you golden-tongued devil, you." She kissed him deeply, soulfully. Neither of them could keep the image of a condemned man having his last meal from their minds.

Michelle put her head on his chest and they lay together for a time. She thought about what she was going to do. She didn't think of anything specific, she just hung up the mental "What am I going to do?" neon sign and let it stay there. He thought about what she said.

Drugs? Gambling? Prostitution? Hey, makes a heck

of a lot of sense, huh? Nothing else did. Was Kao Fei a member of the *Moshuh Nanren* and duty-sworn to kill Daremo? Did the *Moshuh Nanren* support themselves running drugs and women? Or had they been hired to protect Kao Fei? Any way he stacked it, it came out wrong.

If Kao Fei was a magic man, why put out a contract? If Kao Fei hired the magic men as bodyguards, why put out a contract on the bodyguards' foe? Was it all a subterfuge? Was Kao Fei the Figure in Black?

No . . .

Daremo remembered. His mind went back beyond Israel. It went back beyond Iran. It went back to a valley nestled among a circle of volcanoes. It went back to a corpse-strewn campground. It went back to the Figure—the first Figure. It went back to the man he had fought in the terrorist training camp, the one who had run away shouting that the ninjas had yet to pay for crimes against the Liu Chia family.

"Liu Chia."

"What?" Michelle asked sleepily.

"Have you heard the name Liu Chia?"

She sighed, then shrugged, her arms still around him. "I don't know. All these Chinese names sound alike to me. And everybody says them differently. I don't know. Maybe I heard it, but I don't recognize it. I only understand English."

Kao Fei wasn't the Figure in Black. Liu Chia was. Suddenly it made no difference why Kao was trying to kill Daremo. The only thing that mattered was that he was. Daremo didn't need to know *what* the *Moshuh*

Nanren's traps were. He just needed to know *where* they were. Now he knew.

Now he could sleep. The confusions that had been troubling his addled brain had been absorbed. Jumbled memories of Israel had found new homes and settled in. They no longer caused him pain. His mind was clear. He took the beautiful woman in his arms—the one who was near to slumber herself—and closed his eyes.

The blades nearly smashed through his head.

There was a hatchet-topped spear coming from his right, a red-tasseled arrow coming from the left, a straight, two-sided sword coming from the front, a trident coming from the back. If they all met, they would have collided together in the middle of his skull. His head would have exploded like a cantelope filled with cranberry sauce.

But the blades never reached his head. Three more weapons swept them aside. They were huge blades on staffs held by two men and a woman. The trio were Oriental, wearing long, sumptuous costumes with wide sleeves. They had long, flowing hair. The men had long moustaches and beards. They all wore ornate headgear. They stood around him, with their backs to him, protectively. Beyond them was darkness.

Daremo recognized Favorable-Wind Ears instantly.

"I heard you were in trouble," the Hong Kong god said.

"I could see your fate," said Thousand-Mile Eyes.

"We could not allow you to face it alone," said the woman.

"Who are you?" he asked her.

Blades stabbed forward out of the darkness. They stabbed between the gods, trying to destroy Daremo. He ducked as the woman engaged the blade with her own weapon, knocking it up and to the side. It disappeared back into the eternal ink.

"Tin Hau," she said.

"Queen of heaven," said Favorable-Wind.

"Protector of travelers," said Thousand-Mile.

"You are in great danger," she said as all three gods continued to stare away from Daremo as they encircled him. "Greater than you know."

Five blades stabbed from the darkness. The trio fended them off, Thousand-Mile taking two.

Daremo was unimpressed. It was his dream, after all. "Let me help," he said.

"No!" said Tin Hau. "You are not ready. You must train. You must prepare yourself."

"For what?"

"I see Huang Shan," said Thousand-Mile.

"I hear Yenlo Wang," said Favorable-Wind.

"And the Single Sacrifice," said Tin Hau.

"Thanks," said Daremo. "That's a big help."

Tin Hau turned to him, her face enraged, but then her expression softened. "You do not know," she said sadly.

The blade almost split her head in two. Thousand-Mile and Favorable-Wind protected her by making a net of their blades before her face. Two more blades shot at their exposed torsos. Daremo's hands shot up between the gods' bodies, catching the staffs at the end of the enemy blades and throwing them back. The three gods did the rest.

"I know enough," said Daremo. "I'm ready." He was referring to death.

"No!" Tin Hau shouted, turning to him. "No." She let her weapon fall. She slowly, carefully took his head in her hands. She was crying as she kissed him.

The two other gods were attacked. They were forced to either side by the six blades that came from the darkness. They fought in silence.

A spear went through both Tin Hau and Daremo's bodies.

He was torn from her arms. The last thing he saw as he fell was her screaming, tragic face. Then the flames obscured her form. He fell into the flames. They were all around him. But beyond them, there was...something else. The flames were eating away at something. They engulfed something. Something that broke apart in small blazing pieces.

He heard the shrieking from far away. He ignored it, at first, thinking it was Tin Hau. But it wasn't. It was a woman's screams, but they were not those of Tin Hau. They were cries for help, not of loss. Tin Hau would never cry for help. This was not a god screaming.

He rose and moved toward the sound. Soon he could see her figure. It was on fire. He started to run. The figure was screaming, twisting, slapping herself, trying to put out the flames as they engulfed her. It was a pathetic, frightening sight. He ran faster. He had to reach her. He knew that if he reached her he could help her. He could save her.

He ran and he ran. He ran until he could almost make out her features. Something screamed at him. Another voice. From where he had come. It was warning him. But he had to ignore it. She was on fire! She needed his help! He ran forward. The woman was turning toward him, screaming in horror and pain. He put out his hand to touch her.

She turned all the way around.

She faced him.

He recognized her.

He slammed into the Excelsior Hotel window, screaming. The tempered glass held. He was thrown back, his lips and nose bleeding. He fell on his back on the floor, writhing and screaming.

Michelle scrambled out of bed and hugged him, begging him to tell her what was the matter, babbling to him that he was all right.

He stopped shouting. His eyes opened and closed. The hand that was pointing across the bay lowered. He tried, but he couldn't control his breathing, tortured gasps for breath.

Michelle held him to her until his wracking body tremors subsided. She told him everything she was supposed to—"It's all right, I'm here, you're safe"—in different ways and combinations. But when he seemed to calm, her assurances turned to questions.

"What's wrong? What happened, honey?" Her voice was more tender than she thought it could be.

"I . . . I had a nightmare." The voice was small, distant, confused.

"What about?" They weren't just words. She really wanted to know. She didn't know why, but she really wanted to know.

"It was . . . something . . . something . . ."

"What, dear?"

"I . . . don't remember."

Michelle Bowers was to wake up later that night. She was to awaken for just a few seconds. Daremo would be lying beside her. They were enfolded in each other's arms. She would forget the feeling of happiness, but she would remember the rationalization that she only cared because he was her protector—her ticket out of Hong Kong. But she did care.

She kissed him.

She loved him.

7

I'm sorry.

The crying continued.

I'm sorry.

He couldn't say how much. The words meant nothing. Less than nothing in the face of the knowledge.

He could only keep repeating the same thing.

I'm sorry.

The mist rose off the bay that morning. In Victoria Park, the beautifully sculptured garden maintained by the Urban Services League amid the high-rise apartment houses and office buildings, the tai chi classes were exercising—lit by the rising sun.

Tai chi, as a word, represents the yin/yang symbol. The yin/yang symbol represents the flow of positive forces with negative power. The white portion of the teardrop symbol reflects light energy that mingles with the black teardrop portion, which represents dark strength.

The energy is male, the strength female. The two mingle, flow, entwine, encircle. In the writings of Chinese philosophers, life cannot exist without these two forces. More than that, for life to exist, the two forces have to merge. They have to become one.

The tai chi classes exercised as Daremo and Michelle made love. The tai chi students performed their yogalike ritual in the park slowly, delicately, elegantly. They performed the eight hand movements and five foot movements of the skill in a flowing, luxurious dance. The movements caressed the air, combining with each other. The precision of the skill melded with its fluid beauty.

The class ended and the students were dismissed as the two lovers fell into a dreamless sleep. There was much to do today. They all had to prepare for tonight. Tonight was the end of the Seventh Moon. It was the night of Yue Lan.

The Night of the Hungry Ghosts.

Daremo's head was framed in fire. The flames were everywhere.

He walked the streets of Shaukiwan village, between the huts on the hills rising to become Mount Parker and the boats overpopulating the shore. The Tanka boat people who lived in the region raced by him, holding on to their wide-brimmed straw hats. Each one's traditional black pajamalike suit was clearly delineated in the bonfires at every corner.

Shaukiwan was to the north of Causeway, where Kao Fei had an aunt and grandmother. On this holiday night he was certain to visit them.

Daremo smiled at the smallness of the world. Americans had Halloween...

Yes!

... Hong Kong had Yue Lan. The nighttime celebration was named for the keeper of the underworld. Legend had it that once a year, Yue Lan let the ghosts roam the earth for twenty-four hours. The bonfires were made to placate the restless spirits, and food was set out every few feet to feed them—so the passing dead would not consume the living.

Daremo wasn't hungry. He had eaten with Michelle before leaving. Room service had taken care of the meal. They sat on the bed with their chopsticks, partaking of each other's plate. Daremo had the Peking Beggar's Chicken, supposedly invented by a panhandler who had to bury a fowl he had stolen from the emperor. It is wrapped in lotus leaves and baked all day in hot ashes.

Michelle had the Shanghai special Drunken Chicken—a bird cooked in a potent Chinese wine called Shao Shing. They both had Thousand-Year-Old Eggs, which were actually aged in herbs such as arsenic for a few weeks.

"Tastes like sherry," Daremo judged.

"You mean the wine?" Michelle asked, not interested in an answer. "You like?" He nodded, continuing to

pick from his own dish. "We should have gotten seafood. They have great seafood here."

"This is fine."

"You think *this* is fine. They'll cook anything here.
Frogs, snakes, armadillos, anteaters, pigeons, cats . . ."

"Yum," said Daremo, cutting her off and changing
the subject. "What if I tell you Kao Fei couldn't be after
me for drugs."

"I'd say either you were wrong or one of those
fortunetellers he sees told him you'd steal me away."

"I have nothing to do with drugs. I don't care about
drugs."

"You're no fun," she cracked wise. Then she shoveled
a big piece of chicken into her mouth, chewed, swallowed,
then shrugged. "It has to be drugs. He only beats up
and maims people for welching on bets or messing with
his girls."

Michelle ate some more, making the chewing an
exercise that almost rocked the mattress. "The big-time
drug trade has to be responsible for the attacks on you.
They're the only ones with the organization or inclination."

Shrugging off the illogic of Michelle's theory, Daremo
continued his quest to confront Kao Fei. He had no
choice but to follow the snowbirds to ground. Michelle
told him about the holiday and the fishing village just a
few minutes down the east coast.

He extracted a promise from her to stay in the hotel
room. She had wanted to go shopping, but it was too
dangerous. Kao Fei's folks would be looking for both of
them and perhaps even staking out the hotel lobby.

"I'll watch television," she said miserably.

"I thought you didn't know Chinese."

"There are British stations, stupid."

He was stupid, all right. He should not have left her. He should have taken what time he could with her. He wasn't fooling himself. This was not a partnership that would last for eternity. They would grow tired of each other. They were too similar in temperament not to.

That didn't change how they felt at the moment, though. And when the love was that strong and that temporary, it should have been taken advantage of.

She was perfect for Daremo. She was as amoral and uncaring as he. They both lived for the moment, they both had no interests in anything outside themselves, their drives, and their desires. And they were both great in bed.

But Daremo left her. He went to Shaukiwan. He took a tram from the hotel entrance. It was a tall, narrow, low-ceilinged double decker bus that only cost fifty cents. It dropped him right off at the Shing Wong Temple. Outside, children danced in costumes. From inside came the sounds of another Peking Opera performance in progress.

Daremo looked away from the temple. Instead, he looked at the harbor. The shipping fleet there defied count or complete description. There were rowboats, huts on floats, miniature junks with bamboo crosshatched scaffolding, tugboats made from paneling lined with spare tires, shoe-shaped houseboats with thin masts and a clothesline stretched between. The predominant colors were brown for the ships and green for the tarps, curtains, and sails.

All the boats looked like they were on fire as the flames were reflected in the gently rocking sea water. The roads were alive with playing children and entertained adults. Most of the town was inside the temple, enjoying the show. That was where Kao Fei's relatives were as well, no doubt.

The temple was plainly traditional. The roof was green and decorated with sculptures of divinities and good luck charms—not horseshoes or rabbit's feet, but dragons and carps. Daremo walked past the small courtyard, his nostrils filled with the aroma of burning incense. A few feet along was a small altar covered with plates of fruit—sacrifices to the ghosts, he imagined.

Beyond that was the temple's main hall—a large room fronted by a grander altar, a large gold gong, a shrine to Shing Wong, the god of the city, and several funeral displays. The Chinese had teak markers as remembrances of their dead—funeral plaques. Surrounding all this was red brocade inscribed with gold Chinese language characters.

The cavernous hall was empty. The walls were twenty feet on either side of him, as was the ceiling. The sounds of the strident Chinese musical instruments continued to assail his ears, however, and the bonfire light flickered up his back. He slowly walked toward the sounds. He walked around the altar to discover a back courtyard. It was there—surrounded by banyan trees—that the seats, the upraised stage, and the simple white backdrop were set up.

The performers on stage were in the throes of action. All eyes were on the highly stylized and made up actors as they reached a climactic crescendo in their story. Daremo moved casually toward the enthralled audience, confident that no one would notice a round-eye in the back. He could leisurely survey the throng, seeing who matched Michelle's description of Kao Fei. Any major confronting could be done on the Feis' way back home.

As hard as Daremo concentrated on the people in the seats, the people on stage kept distracting him. A character was doing "Monkey"-style kung fu up there. There was Iron Monkey, the brutal attack form, then there was this—the mincing, prancing style where the martial artist practically impersonated a chimp.

The actor danced and tumbled, his body flying around in the air, his footwork constantly changing. He was dressed in a red, black, and orange tunic and dark tan pants. On his head was a matching dark tan turban. But it was his face that was the most interesting. His face had been painted white. And on that white visage had been painted a red mask with black lines.

The red section went around the eyes, around the nose, and then straight down across the mouth and chin in two bands. A two-tongued fork of black was painted just below the nose, and more black, waving lines were painted on the cheeks and the forehead. The actor had been made up to look like a cartoon monkey.

The other actor onstage seemed to be a Chinese version of the burly, bewhiskered villains Charlie Chaplin used to fight. For this performance, the character was in ornate black and white. He wore a huge gown of interwoven black and white patterns and a white headdress with long black plumes. His face was painted white with some minimal black lines, but his chin and mouth were obscured by a huge, bushy moustache and beard, which hung down to his stomach.

The only other color Daremo could see was a bright red tassel that hung from the actor's ear to his waist. The Monkey man carried a long, thin black-and-white-striped pole, while the bearded fellow had a legendary weapon—a long staff ending in a horizontal quarter-moon blade. The two encircled each other, their legs making one pattern while their hands made another, twirling their implements in a combination fight and baton performance.

As before, the effect was charming—in spite of the dissonant, raucous music consisting of drum and cymbal clashes. Every few seconds, the Monkey would get the advantage of the blustering bearded one, then strike a specific one-legged pose with one hand skyward as the music stopped and the crowd laughed and applauded.

Daremo smiled. He concentrated on the crowd, picking out each audience member as if his eyes were thirty-five millimeter cameras. His concentration was almost immediately broken by the end of the onstage scene and the sudden appearance of dancing demons.

They came from all around him—from backstage, from behind the banyan trees. They surrounded the audience and danced down the center aisle. They tumbled, flipped, somersaulted, cartwheeled, and twirled on the stage and on the temple grounds. It was an impressive display of gymnastics that swirled before Daremo's eyes.

They were all young men and women in costumes. The Monkey and bearded fighter had disappeared, but garish, painted images of devils and demons were now being hung from the stage backdrop and the surrounding trees. More demons ran in from the temple proper with torches in their hands. It was time to send the roaming ghosts back to hell. Their twenty-four hours were up. Their images would be purged in an exorcism of fire.

It was cause for renewed celebration. The crowd cheered and toasted the demons with cups of tea and glasses of wine. Both the tea and wine were drunk from tiny round cups, like handsomely decorated, handleless espresso cups. The tea was poured from ceramic and brass pitchers, but the wine was in small clay jugs covered with dark red paper.

The crowd began to chant in support of the ritual. Daremo tried to move back to keep away from the action as much as possible, but the dancing demons hemmed him in. The chant got louder and louder as the demons pulled swords and spears from their tunics and danced in a martial pattern. The torches would be brought closer to the effigies and the chanting would grow louder. The torches would be pulled away and the chants would dim.

"Yue Lan, Yue Lan, Yue Lan, Yue Lan," the crowd chanted as the dance continued. Soon the chant took on a life of its own. The torch position no longer had an effect. The crowd chanted louder and louder, becoming more and more insistent.

"Yue Lan, Yue Lan, Yue Lan, Yue Lan!"

First, Daremo smelled the trouble. Mingled with the stinging torch smoke fumes, the sweet wine aroma, and the pungent tea smell was the slight whiff of gasoline. Daremo looked quickly around, crouched, then almost ran toward the seated audience.

Next, he heard it. He heard it twice over in his mind.

He heard Michelle. "All these Chinese names sound alike to me."

He heard Favorable-Wind Ears. "I hear Yenlo Wang."

He said it the way Daremo would read the name. Yen-low Wang. Yenlo Wang.

Yenlowang, yenlowang, yenlowan.

Yelowan, ye-lo-wan, yelwan.

Yeulan, yuelan, yue-lan, Yue Lan, Yue Lan, Yue Lan!

"Yue Lan, Yue Lan, Yue Lan!" the crowd shrieked.

The god of hell, Yenlo, pronounced Yue in Cantonese, Wang, pronounced Lan in Cantonese.

The gods had been trying to tell him something, all right. Why didn't the gods ever talk straight?

Look, stupid, a bunch of bozos are going to try to kill you on Yue Lan.

Thanks a lot, guys.

Daremo dove into the last aisle of the audience as the oil was hurled at him. The liquid splashed across the back of the seats as Daremo slid between the legs of the people in the last row and the legs of the chairs in the second to last row. He crawled like a snake on the ground, the people complaining at first, then laughing.

A demon ran around to meet Daremo at the other end of the row. Daremo leaped up in the middle of the row, threw his legs out in a midair split over the heads of those in the last row, and then landed behind their chairs.

Two demons raced at him from either side. He waited until they were almost on him, then spun brutally around, his open hands sweeping out from his hips. There were two cracks, as if two wooden paddles had struck a tree trunk, then the two demons flew backward and Daremo's arms snapped back to his side.

The powerful Hsing-I blows erupted from Daremo as an external explosion of his internal rage. Traps on traps on traps. Had the *Moshuh Nanren* guessed he'd be here or was he led? Had he fought off four assassination attempts or were those people sacrifices to lead him here?

No matter, no difference. He was here and they were springing their trap, a trap lined with innocent bystanders and flaming effigies. All the mock-up figures had been set on fire. The musicians played with energetic fervor. The demons danced with renewed frenzy, contorting as if the flames were inside them, pulling them back to hell in a bone-breaking whirlpool. Amid the noise and contortions, Daremo's fight was unnoticeable.

But not for long. Daremo ran down the center aisle, pushing demons out of his way and onto the audience members seated on the aisle. He didn't even slow when the demon closest to the stage whirled to meet him, his sword arcing downward. The entire audience gasped as the blade seemed to meet Daremo's upraised arm, but his hand was gripping the *tanto* and its short blade was against the sharp edge of the sword.

He swirled the sword away from his limb and face, his own leg becoming a sword of sorts itself. He executed the visually stunning, extremely difficult front twisting kick to the swordman's head. He moved his leg up straight, to the left of the swordsman, then curved, twisted to the right, slamming the top of his into the man's ear and temple, hurling him to the ground.

The crowd loved it. They also loved his leaping somersault onto the stage as the demons charged him from either side. They loved the way he was fighting even as he landed, slamming the dancing devils on the stage with both hands as he moved toward the rear of the platform.

The demons thrust their blades and spears at him, but he slashed the *tanto* in blindingly fast patterns to fend off the attacks. Still, they had slowed him down. The sheer mass of weapons against him soon stopped his forward progress. He was stuck midstage with at least four men facing him and more leaping onstage behind him.

The empty 7.62 gun came out of his pocket. The demons were too hopped up to care. That was all right. Daremo was planning to use it as a defensive weapon. He was not a master of the mythical Toad or Spiritual or Gaseous Armor form of kung fu, which supposedly made the skin impervious to blades. He could protect himself just so long with the *tanto*. He used the mental automatic as his blocking blade for two-handed defense.

His legs, arms, and the rest of his body were his offensive weapons. Daremo swirled onstage, the clash of metal sending off sparks. He ducked, crouched, dove, and twisted, his legs lashing out, catching men in the knees, crotch, stomach, neck and face with his own feet, knees, elbows, and head.

The *ki* energy flowed within him, effortlessly pulling knowledge from his subconscious mind, feeding it through his conscious mind to his limbs. He was almost watching himself perform the miraculous kung fu battle. He was hardly recognizing anything he did. The new channels in his brain were greasing the mind's already extraordinary processes as if he were on automatic pilot.

It left his mind free to consider strategy. He could not keep this stage show up for long. It was giving the demons a place to congregate. He would soon be overwhelmed by sheer numbers. Daremo hit a swordman in the face with the gun. He let the gun go and ripped the straight Chinese *wu tang* sword from the man's hand as he fell. The others came at him with their broad-bladed, curved tai chi swords.

It was Zorro unchained! Daremo swung the sword as if he had been reunited with a masterful friend, sending the demons back, accompanied by the cheers of the audience. They had no idea what the battle between the round-eye and the demons represented, but they were enjoying the pure drama of it.

As the devils reeled away, Daremo saw the wine jugs that had been placed on the stage. He fought toward them, jabbing and twisting the blade as if it were an extension of his arm. He fought toward the front of the stage while the effigies burned behind him at the backdrop.

A sudden feint and a blinding side karate kick—which

sent a demon flying into the air, jackknifed, into the middle aisle, on his back. Daremo made room for himself with the swinging *tanto*, then jammed the sword through the red paper top and into the wine jug. The welcome aroma of gasoline assailed his nostrils. Then the demons tried to.

He splashed gas into their faces with a swing of the sword, kept others back with a simultaneous wide slash of the *tanto*, then dipped the sword back into the fuel. He flung the excess off the blade into the eyes of others before jamming the tip into the jug a third time. Then he picked up the jug with the blade and hurled it toward a burning effigy at the backdrop.

One poor devil who was not blinded by the gasoline leaped to intercept the spinning, spilling jug. Daremo hurled the *tanto* into the man's chest. The devil kept going, but his hands were weakened by the mortal wound. The jug shot between his clutching arms and hit him in the face. The clay shattered. The man's body flew back, his head in the middle of a cloud of gasoline.

A single spark from the effigy lit the mixture and the devil head exploded in midair.

The audience shrieked. The body slammed into the backdrop, completing the flame connection. The fire ripped along the network of spilled gasoline, setting the backdrop ablaze. The demons were distracted by the sudden inferno. That was all Daremo needed.

He charged through them. He hurled three men aside before he was able to stick his sword into the consuming flame. When he spun to face the demons again, he was holding a fire sword. He raised the burning blade to the heavens.

They ran. They retreated through the audience, who had risen to their feet as one. The exploding head had been too much. Many women had already been taken out. Others had fainted and were being tended to. The crowd yelled its delight and displeasure. Meanwhile, the show must go on.

Daremo cut down those demons immediately in front of him. He stepped forward to swing the flaming blade into the faces of those he had splashed with gasoline. Some fell with their skin rent. Others fell with their faces and hair aflame. Daremo ran to the edge of the stage. A man leaped up, his spear ripping through Daremo's shirt.

He was taken completely by surprise, much to his amazed shame. He had not seen or sensed the man crouching there. The tip of the spear touched Daremo's stomach. But it was not too late. He was prepared to hurl his body up and away from the spear. But then a horizontal half-moon blade appeared, catching the spearhead at its base and pushing the weapon away. Daremo swung his sword down and sliced open the demon's skull.

He looked over to see the bearded villain with the black and white face pulling his legendary weapon back to his side.

"*Um goi*," he said to the man. The bearded one ran from him, seemingly in terror. He disappeared through a slit in the burning backdrop. He was more willing to face the flames than Daremo.

Daremo followed him. He had no choice. The stunned, disgusted audience was just beginning to realize that the deaths had not been special effects. As realistic and shocking as those deaths were, the people could not accept that a real life-and-death struggle had been played out with gymnastics, kung fu, and swords before their eyes. They were used to shoot-outs and car chases. They were used to armies of cops surrounding an area until the villain was gunned down. They were only used to battles like this in Shaw Brothers or Golden Harvest cinemas.

Daremo threw back the backdrop curtain. The performers were gone. All he saw was the back wall of the temple courtyard. A few feet away from a wooden stair connecting the stage with the ground was an open gate. He ran outside the temple walls, closing the wrought-iron gate door after him.

The aftermath of a trap. What was he going to do? Fly home? Daremo, the fight descriptions aside, was no caped superhero. He had little choice but to return to the bus stop and wait for the next tram. It was only a matter of minutes and the bus driver knew nothing of the in-town fuss. Daremo kept his eyes open for any sign of the police, who had to have been called in by now.

He didn't have the gun, the *tanto*, or the sword anymore. But they would find no fingerprints on them. He didn't have any.

He got back to Causeway Bay without incident and without any comments about his ripped shirt. He walked carefully into the hotel and moved to the stairway. He could see no one waiting or watching for him. He walked up the steps to the floor his room was on. He walked silently down the hall to the door. He listened carefully, his fingers on the obstruction.

He heard nothing and no one inside. Michelle could be sleeping... or Michelle could be waiting. Or Michelle could be dead. What Michelle couldn't be was a dupe, a double, a traitor. Not that it wasn't possible that a white woman was a Chinese magician/spy. Hell, if he could be a ninja, she could be *Monshuh Feh Neu*—magic woman. Hell, if *he* could be a ninja, so could *she*.

But she had had plenty of opportunities to kill him. He had been asleep in her arms twice. Unless Kao Fei or Liu Chia or whoever had a *specific* reason to want him dead in Shaukiwan, her role as informant didn't make sense. It had to be the way it appeared to be. They were trying to kill him. He had pulled her from a hooker hell. She was grateful.

What she wasn't was in the room. But there were no little twerps in jackets and sunglasses with guns either. There was a note. It was written in English. It said that if he wanted to see the girl ever again, come to the Tiger Balm Gardens at noon tomorrow.

Daremo went downstairs and bought a new shirt in the lobby's twenty-four-hour store. The chattering salesclerk wanted him to have a nice light blue or white silk shirt, but he wanted something dark and simple. The best he could get was a dark blue light cotton shirt. He tucked it into the denims and asked about Michelle.

The salesclerk didn't remember seeing anyone of that

description. neither did the desk man. *Don't question:
accept*. Kao Fei had searched for her, found out she was
staying at the Excelsior by asking around (who was
going to not notice an American blonde?), staked out
the place until the very dangerous man left, then sent
demons after him and kidnappers after her.

When the demons fucked up, Kao Fei had probably
left the little village and his relatives, returned ahead of
Daremo, and left the note. He probably had a private
car. He had probably been in the room while Daremo
was making tram stops at Sai Wan Ho, Quarry Bay, and
North Point. Daremo paid the salesclerk and left the
hotel.

The clouds were already beginning to gather that
morning. It was still dark when Signal One went out.

Daremo walked past the central market as the produce sellers prepared for their six A.M. opening. He
walked down Cloth Alley, filled with fabric store after
tailor shop after cleaners. He walked down Wing Sing
Street, also known as Egg Street.

He passed the snake shops on Hillier Street and the
antique stores on Cat Street. He passed the Man Mo
Temple on Hollywood Road. Man Mo is actually the
god of civil servants.

He walked into Happy Valley. By then the wind was
beginning to pick up and the sun was mugged by
black-lined clouds waiting to ambush it at the horizon.
Daremo passed the Happy Valley Racecourse, where
nags made the rounds every weekend. Beyond lay
three acres of garish bad taste: the Tiger Balm Gardens.

Aw Woon Par, an eccentric philanthropist, built the place in 1935 for a cost of sixteen million Hong Kong dollars. The cure-all medication he invented was tiger balm. No one much remembers the stuff now, but it was big in the sixties for "curing" head and muscle aches.

Tiger Balm Gardens was a latterday nightmare. It had been pretty grotesque when it was opened decades ago but was all the more ludicrous now by its state of disrepair. The plants were overgrown with weeds, and the statues and dioramas showing scenes from Chinese legend and history were crumbling. It had become a prime location for drug deals.

If Michelle's feelings were correct, the Tiger Gardens was a perfect place for a meeting between a drug crime lord and whoever they thought Daremo was. They obviously didn't think he was a ninja.

Who *did* they think they were dealing with? "If you want to see the girl alive again..." Who cares? Who cares? What did they think? That he didn't notice they didn't ask for any money? What did they think? That he'd just walk in "tomorrow at noon" with the stiff upper lip and jutting jaw, hoping to tough it out?

"I don't care what you do to me, just leave the girl alone..."

"Let the girl go. She has nothing to do with this!"

"This is between you and me, Fei. Let the girl go."

It is to laugh. Or barf.

Daremo did an exhaustive exploration of the gardens, hours before it opened. The only thing that fazed him at all were the scenes of people being tortured in hell—bodies impaled on spikes, disembodied heads. The pure, undiluted bad taste of the stone tableaux didn't bother him. It just reminded him of something else.

When his killers started appearing out of fancy cars to take their places in the park, he waited until they were settled and took them out, one by one. He whispered the same thing in each one's ear before he punched out his heart.

One guy had a silenced .22 pistol. Another had a Type 56 carbine. Another had a Type 68 rifle. One even had a Type 56-1 assault rifle modeled on the Russian AK-47. They were local professional help—Not a single white or black face in the bunch. Is this the way the Chinese didn't take any chances? Driving up to the rendezvous in BMWs and Mercedeses? Carrying their weapons in suitcases? Hiding in bushes **and** behind trees?

To their credit, they did place a bunch of "undercover" assassins on the benches and walking the paths. Daremo ignored them as he waltzed over to each hidden hitman.

"Where's the girl?" *Wham*.

"Where's the girl?" *Crunch*.

"Where's the girl?" *Crack*.

."Where's the girl?" *Stab*.

"Where's the girl?"

"In the Walled City." *Gag*. "At Fei's place." *Choke*.

"Thank you." *Bash*.

8

Signal Three was out by the time he returned to Hong Kong Harbor. There was no signal Two. There used to be, but there wasn't anymore.

The black ball was flying high, buffeted by the wind, on the pole overlooking the little sampans and walla-wallas still lashed to underwater uprights.

Daremo couldn't get the ferry, and the MTR wasn't running. Neither were the buses, taxis, trains, or trams, but those hardly made any difference. They couldn't get him to Kowloon.

He stood in the heavy rain, yelling down at the sailors. *"Look yat pak negan!"*

"Mao, mao, mao," an old man holding on to the pier for balance yelled back, shaking his head. He kept pointing at the black ball on the pole as if the round-eye were blind.

"*Yat tsin ngan!*" Daremo shouted to anyone who'd listen. The price had just gone from six hundred to a thousand dollars. That changed the old man's attitude. Instead of pointing to the black ball, he pointed to the upside down *T* on another pole.

Daremo was about to up the ante again when a young man ran up alongside and beat him to it. He shouted at the seafarers as the ninja opened his mouth.

"Signal Eight!" That got some action. The men scrambled out of their craft and ran across the pier. Daremo watched them disappear into the thick of the torrential rain as the young man in the gray slicker pulled the upside down *T* from the pole and replaced it with a triangle.

"What's the problem?" Daremo asked him.

The young man stared at him and chuckled. "You drunk or something? Look around you."

Daremo did as he was told. "So it's raining."

"It's monsoon, man," the Oriental said. "Signal Eight."

"What's that?"

"What's that? It's the signal after signal Three."

"What happened to signals four through seven?"

"Too complicated. The government simplified it." The man started walking away. "You better get inside."

Daremo grabbed his arm. "Two thousand dollars if you take me across."

The Oriental just looked at him. "You are crazy, man. Don't you know when to come out of the rain?"

"Here," Daremo said, taking all the money out of his pocket. "Name your price." He looked at the soggy bills. "You'll have to dry them out, though," he said wearily.

The man pulled his arm free, curling his lip in disgust. "There are some things you can't buy, *gwailo*," he spat, using the ancient term for "foreign devil." "When are you bastards going to learn that?" He walked away.

Daremo was left in the howling wind and battering rain. The day was called on account of a Signal-Eight typhoon. He looked back toward the boats rocking on the choppy seas. He looked down at the soggy, disintegrating bills in his palm. He turned his hand over and let the sodden wad of paper fall into the harbor like a stone.

Daremo walked to the pier, found the sturdiest walla-walla he could, and started across the bay. Why hadn't he thought of this before? Because he had been having trouble thinking ever since finding the ransom note. He didn't know why he was even bothering with Michelle Bowers. He should be wringing the next piece of the puzzle out of Kao Fei.

But here he was trying to cross Hong Kong Harbor. The Star Ferry took seven minutes to make the trip. Daremo took almost seventy—having to zigzag across the heavy seas, restart the engine when it conked out, and row when the machine died out completely.

Fifty feet off the Kowloon shore, the boat capsized and sank. Daremo swam the rest of the way, his clothes dragging at his limbs. He climbed out of the surf roughly where his second assassin had climbed up and pushed himself through the empty streets.

He passed the YMCA and the ritzy Peninsula Hotel, sitting side by side on Salisbury Street. He kept moving deeper and deeper into Tsimshatsui until he found a clothing store that wasn't occupied by a family. He broke the door down and pulled what he needed off the shelves. He left his old clothes as collateral.

The figure that moved back onto the flooded streets was in black and blue. The blue, thankfully, was a plastic raincoat with hood. That helped with the rain, but not at all with the wind. The close-knit skyscrapers that made up Kowloon created natural channels for the air to be sucked into. Even Daremo was stopped dead in his tracks several times.

But he kept going until he was on the outskirts of the Walled City of Kowloon. There was no more wall. The Japanese had used it to build an airport runway when they had occupied China during World War Two. The walls had been erected in the first place during the nineteenth century to keep at least a small part of Hong Kong fiercely Chinese after the British occupation.

That pride went with the wall. It was now just Kowloon's slum. Two- and four-story buildings huddled together, seemingly just to keep upright. Everything was brown brick, black stone, and gray concrete, unlike the pearly white remainder of the city. All around the buildings, crammed into whatever spaces they could find, were tin shacks and corrugated squatter's huts—Or what was left of them after the typhoon wind got through.

Daremo struggled down the main road, Boundary Street, until he found an open doorway. He almost fell inside, breathing deeply and spitting out the water that was coursing between his clenched teeth. The hall was like almost any other ghetto hall anywhere else in the world. It was narrow, it was crumbling, it was dark, and it smelled.

Daremo leaned against the wall, his head up. He had no choice. He could no longer use his body to find her. Kao Fei's "place," as the assassin had called it, was not to be found on foot. Daremo had the address, but the address could be anywhere. There were no street signs in the Walled City, and he hadn't had time to ask detailed directions.

He had to use his mind. He had to risk the mind-bridge. She was important enough. Wasn't she? He didn't know what he felt anymore. He just knew he had to find her.

Daremo closed his eyes. And thought.

Where is she?
I do not know.
Is she all right?
I do not know.
She lives.
And will die. Like everyone.
You . . . *gwailo,* you.
Remember the feeling. Feel it again.
Feel it.
Love.
Yes . . .
Love.

The Figure in Black fell to his knees in the alley. He gripped the sides of his head. He nearly collapsed. He was on all fours, gasping for a few seconds as the rain slammed on him. He had to pull his hood off quickly so he wouldn't throw up in it

The junkie almost got him. He almost got the rusty kitchen knife into his side.

Daremo came out of it just in time. He awoke to find his eyes full of the sweating face and greasy black hair.

He grabbed the wrist, then twisted and squeezed at the same time. The man was about to shriek in pain as he dropped the weapon, but Daremo hit him hard in the stomach.

The man wheezed, the cry cut off. Daremo put his hand around the man's neck, just under the addict's chin.

"That's the second time in two days!" Daremo hissed. He threw the man three feet off the ground and into the opposite wall.

The wall cracked under the man's weight and the power of Daremo's throw. The emaciated Oriental slid down to the floor. He sat in the hall, groaning. Daremo kicked him in the face with the flat of his foot. He crushed the man's skull with a savage blow. The junkie fell over sideways, his lungs' last air making a tiny whistling sound in the tenement.

He deserved it, Daremo thought. That was the second time on this trip that someone nearly knifed him. He was getting tired of this shit. What was he doing? What the fuck was he doing?

Daremo stumbled out the door. He let his mind take

control. His feet moved to where his mind led them. He went around the corner, ran down the narrow side street, and made a left into an alley.

He instantly fell onto his back, right into a puddle, making a splash. The *shuriken* thrown by the Figure in Black soared over his head. He rolled to the left, toward an open window. He became part of a waterfall that coursed down the basement wall. He ran along the wall, following the Figure's progress in the street-level windows.

He ran to the crooked, rotting cellar steps and jumped to the first floor. He emerged in a large corner room. It had seen better times. There was no furniture and no fixtures—just holes in the wall where they used to be. Water streamed in from at least a dozen cracks in the ceiling. The Figure was framed in the large window for a second before he ran.

Daremo leaped through the broken glass to follow him. The Figure had already turned the corner at the far end of a muddy courtyard. Daremo was about to follow him when—

Love.

He had felt it. He had felt it coming from somewhere.

It was not repeated. Daremo carefully looked around. He looked up. In a room on the second story of a building were shadows.

Michelle Bowers lay on her back on the floor. Her hands were over her head. Her wrists were crossed and tied so tightly to a pipe in the wall that her skin was torn and bleeding.

Her dress had been torn up and wrapped inside, and then around, her mouth. Her hair had been yanked out from under the cloth and then the gag had been knotted behind her head.

A rope was wrapped around each of her ankles. A one-foot length of cord stretched from each ankle to her thighs. The rope was tied around each thigh, so her knees were bent.

She lay in a puddle of rain water, sweat, and her own urine. Each of the four men there took turns raping her. One was on her now, slobbering on her neck, grinding her breasts beneath his hands, and thrusting inside her.

He only stopped when the door to the second-story room fell in.

Daremo held on to the sides of the doorway for support. He looked into the corner room. The ceiling was twelve feet high. There was a side window looking out into the alley. There was a window on the back wall that looked out into the courtyard. Michelle's hands were just below that. The other three men sat around her like camping boy scouts, their guns at their sides.

"Do you know me?" Daremo said, walking in. They just stared at him as if he were a mirage and brought up their guns level with his approaching chest.

They couldn't understand his English words. But he kept walking and he kept talking.

"That's why I carry these," he said, holding out his open palms for them to see. "My name," he said, "is trouble." He fell through the floor.

The men around the girl leaped to their feet in

surprise. The man on top of Michelle just did a push-up and looked over at the hole in the wooden slats. The rotting floor had given way.

The man closest to the hole leaned over and looked through the floor. He turned his head to the others. "He's not down there," he said.

Then two fists came through the floor on either side of his left leg. The fingers clamped together around his ankle. Then the man also fell through the floor. The man on top of Michelle rolled off and scrambled for his gun. He was making so much noise doing it that it even distracted the two guys who were standing.

The man who had been on top of Michelle managed to grab his gun just as a bullet went through the floor and into his chest. He opened his mouth to cry out, but his lips just twisted off his teeth in pain before he collapsed.

The remaining two men spun around to him and then back to the holes in the floor. They pointed their guns down and shot up the first floor's ceiling. Each fired three rounds, and then they waited to see if there was any response. There was. The wall three feet down from the door fell in.

Daremo came through the hole in the wall, gun first. He shot one man in the head, and then the other. The first man fell backward. The second man fell forward, onto the two holes. His weight connected the dots, making one big hole as he fell through.

Daremo dropped the gun he had taken from the man he had pulled through the floor. He went to Michelle and carefully untied her. She didn't say anything when he pulled the cloth from her mouth. She didn't cry. She tried to wrap her arms around him, but she was too weak.

Instead, he held her. He held her while her limbs started gaining strength. His face was in her hair. Her head was against his chest. She could hear his heart beating.

They just stayed in the corner of the room until the wind stopped blowing and the water stopped dripping from the cracks in the ceiling. They didn't say or do anything. Daremo just thought.

Love.

Again and again and again.

But she did not hear.

The typhoon was over. Hong Kong came out from shelter and tentatively blinked toward the lightening sky. The clouds began to float away. The taxis and trains and ferries started running again. Stores opened for business. The inner workings of the Hong Kong financial district picked up speed. You know the worst is really over when the hookers come out again. The hookers came out again.

It would be a good night for Kao Fei. The Oriental with the strong, wide face, the thick lips, and the sharp eyes made himself a drink. It had better be a good night, at least financially. He needed that money. He needed it to rebuild the shambles of his organization. He hardly had a bodyguard left after what the American had done.

It didn't seem possible. Only in town for two days

and the unarmed Anglo had decimated most of Fei's inner and outer staff. Too bad his people had to postpone the Tiger Balm Gardens hit because of the storm. They weren't able to signal all the gunmen, but these guys knew enough to get out of the rain. They had sure cost enough to know.

Fei was certain that the hitmen would call in as soon as the phone lines were repaired, and his stoolies would soon spot the ugly American again. How hard would it be to locate one dour round-eye? The police wouldn't be looking for him—not if Fei's information was correct.

The vice lord took stock. The Bowers girls was safely tucked away, so the round-eye was still on the hook. Master killer or not, he still wanted that girl. So all Kao Fei had to do was reschedule Daremo's Tiger Balm demise.

It couldn't be too soon for me, he thought as he walked across the room lit by the early evening sun. This guy wasn't worth all the trouble. If it wasn't for . . . well, for that other stuff, Fei would have thrown up a white flag and talked a deal half a day ago. He was just lucky that the round-eye hadn't cornered him at the office or the Yue Lan celebration. That was something, at least. At least he, Kao Fei, was safe.

"Hey, man," said Daremo.

Kao Fei whirled around, dropping his drink on the plush carpet. Behind the bar stood an American. He could just be made out in the diffused sunset light coming through the picture window and the rich yellow curtains.

"You've been wasting my time," said Daremo.

Fei just stared at him, then made a jump for the coffee table. Daremo moved. Fei's wrist was pinioned, his fingers inches from the alarm button. He was locked into place by his own ice tongs, sunk two inches into the thick coffee table top. They vibrated around his wrist like an angry rattlesnake. The Oriental looked back at Daremo in shock.

"Who are you?" A whisper.

Daremo shrugged his shoulders in mirth. "Nobody."

It was too incredible. "How did you get in?"

Daremo took an ice cube from the silver bucket and broke it on the bar top. He moved. Kao Fei felt something sting his face.

"You're wasting my time again."

He moved. Another sting.

"What do you want?" Kao Fei begged as the blood began to dribble down his forehead and chin.

"Why are you trying to kill me?" He ignored Fei's incredulous face. "Just tell me."

Fei looked all over the room for some sort of assistance. He was bent over, his hand trying to pull out from under the ice tongs. He suddenly realized that his other hand was free. He slapped it down on the alarm button while yelling.

"Help! Somebody help me, please!"

Nothing happened.

Daremo moved twice. Two more stings. The first dart had melted and was making teardrops down Fei's face. "Why are you trying to kill me?"

Kao Fei inhaled sharply. "You're a threat to my organization!" he yelled.

"Who told you that?"

Kao Fei just stared. "You're an Interpol drug agent."

Daremo smirked. He hefted the rest of the shattered ice cube in his hand, then dropped it on the floor. He came around the bar and approached Kao Fei—in his beautiful silk suit, in his beautiful hilltop home in the Peak Towers development near Mount Gough—lord of the Wanchai.

Daremo stopped directly in front of him. "Who told you that?"

Kao Fei stared at the American in defiance.

Daremo looked at the stubborn man evenly. Then he stepped on Kao Fei's foot, breaking nearly every bone. Fei started to drop to the floor, but Daremo held him by the neck in a grip that kept him upright and awake through the astonishing pain.

"Who told you that?"

"Liu Chia," Kao Fei gasped.

"Where is he?"

Kao Fei wheezed and snorted.

"Where is he?"

Kao Fei summoned up all his courage and all his strength. He spit on Daremo's shirt. He didn't have the strength to aim the mucus any higher.

Daremo just smiled.

"Let me introduce you to the joys of internal bleeding," he said.

Michelle Bowers sat in the King's Park Hotel room. She sat at the desk. She had a pen in her hand. She stared through the piece of paper. She felt nothing.

She heard a noise at the door. She looked over.
The Figure in Black walked in.

Daremo found the note when he returned. It was
written in longhand on hotel stationery.
"Why I became a hooker" was the title.

> I don't know. It seemed the best thing to do
> at the time. I didn't have enough interest to do
> any regular jobs. I didn't have enough brains to
> do anything exciting. I didn't have enough talent
> to act or sing or dance. I didn't even have enough
> height to become a model. All I had was a body.
> But everybody loved that.
>
> Thanks for getting me out of the hole. I've got
> enough money to catch a plane somewhere.
>
> I don't know what else to say. Don't worry about
> me.
>
> Love,
> P.S. I got this for you. Everybody wears them.

On the bottom of the sheet of paper was a circular
piece of jade, a little round ring—the symbol for heaven
in Chinese mythology.
Daremo left the hotel. He left Hong Kong. He left
Kowloon. He went north.

The King's Park Hotel.
An empty room.
There's a sound at the door. The maid comes in.
She dusts. She vacuums. She cleans the bathroom.

She replaces the soap and towels. She makes the bed. She empties the trashcan into the plastic bag on her cart.

She doesn't notice the crumbled sheet of paper.

Part Three

Smiling, sincere, incorruptible—
His body disciplined and limber.
A man who had become what he
    could,
And was what he was—
Ready at any moment to gather
    everything
Into one simple sacrifice.

Dag Hammarskjold

9

What had she done? Walked naked from her slum prison in the Walled City to the King's Park Hotel? No, of course not. She had worn the blue slicker he had stolen. And once they got back to downtown Kowloon, they bought her another outfit from the money they had taken from her.

What did Daremo do? Look up Kao Fei's name in the phone book? That's exactly what he did. He looked up Kao Fei, Kao Fei Industries, the Tulip Bar, and the names of several other Fei-owned shops and establishments she had been aware of. She also knew he had a house somewhere on Peak Towers. Hell, all the girls knew that. They made jokes about it.

He found the place, found and cut the buried alarm wires, waltzed right in and silently eradicated every guard, then went to read the riot act to Kao Fei himself. No problem. His mind was like a whip. When he had seen what they did to her, it snapped taut. When he returned to the hotel to get her, it started to unravel.

He could imagine her sitting there, "composing" her goodbye note. He could see the ideas come streaming out in the first few lines and her rush to write them down before the mental images and perceptions disappeared from her brain like water being absorbed by parched desert sand. Then he could see the pause between the line about her body and the thank you. Then he could see the pauses between the lines getting longer and longer.

What to say, what to say. "I don't know what to say." That was brave of her. She had eliminated all the possible lies and fantasies to write down the truth. "I don't know what to say." What could she say? Could she say that she had been treated as a thing all her life? Could she say that everyone, including herself, started treating her differently when her sides curved and her breasts grew?

Could she say she started becoming the thing others seem to want her to become? Could she say she started treating others the same way? Could she say she stopped taking anything seriously, including herself? Because if she took herself seriously, she'd have to take who and what she was seriously, and she didn't know who or what that was. Could she say she loved him? No, because she didn't. She didn't love herself—how could she love him?

Naw, she couldn't say any of that. It sounded too

stupid. Even written out this way, it sounds too stupid, too street-corner psychoanalytic.

What could she say? She could say goodbye. What could she do? Not think about it.

But all he could do was think about it. Later, he rationalized that was all he could do on the boring train trip through the new Territories. He sat on the Kowloon/Canton Railway, staring at the passing countryside, thinking about how stupid it sounded.

Mongkok, first stop on the local train: What did he care? He didn't love himself either, so how could he love her?

Kowloon Tong, second stop: He didn't love her, he couldn't. He just loved the companionship, the affection, the sex.

Shatin, third stop: He hadn't had sexual relations since Israel, and that was all technique. All he had wanted to do was control Rachel Assaf.

Chinese University, fourth stop: There were plenty of recriminations he had to whip himself with about Israel and the Season of Sand. He simply couldn't believe how heinous he was.

Tai Po Kau: Ninja or no, the human body was set up a certain way. Sex was natural, sex was necessary, sex was desirable, sex was needed. He could try to ignore it, but what was he going to do with these hormones?

Fanling: She was better off this way. What was he going to do, bring her along? Send her to the States and ask her to wait for him? Totally ridiculous. What was the problem here? She was a fucking whore, for God's sake. What was he all worked up about? Good riddance!

So why the hell couldn't he get her out of his mind? What was going on up there?

Sheung Shui, last stop. Last stop, that is, for anybody who didn't have a visa to enter the People's Republic of China. The border town of Lo Wu was next, and while acquiring a Chinese visa was a fairly simple maneuver in these enlightened times, Daremo no longer had a passport to acquire one with. Nor did he have the facilities to forge one.

So he got off the train and breathed the clean air of the New Territory town on the border of the great frontier. The Next Territories were the waystations between the People's Republic and Hong Kong. The New Territories became necessary because the mainland Chinese were taking back Hong Kong from the British when the Limeys' lease ran out in 1997.

All the towns between became a buffer for the communist Republic and the imperialist HK—the way Hong Kong had originally been a buffer between China and the rest of the world. Daremo walked the streets of this second to last town before the border, vainly attempting to maintain his previous, much vaunted, amoral objectivity.

Things were quieter, less crowded, here than they were in Hong Kong proper. The streets were wider, but there was more dust and dirt. Even so, it was off-white, silken sandlike dust that stretched from concrete to concrete wall. There was enough room to move, but people still sold fresh vegetables and fish from street stalls.

The smell of the sea permeated the entire Tolo

Harbor Coast—the harbor on the other side of the Hong Kong Harbor, the harbor to the east of the Kowloon peninsula—the way the smell of tomato sauce permeates South Philadelphia. Although Sheung Shui was a few meters up from the edge of the Tolo harbor, seafood was still plentiful, inexpensive, and in demand.

Daremo froze in his tracks in the center of the village. He moved slowly toward the town hall. Slowly, he read the Cantonese and English signs outside proclaiming it to be the council hall dating back to 1751. History says it was once the main ancestral home of the Liu clan, who established the town in the thirteenth century.

Coincidence? Probably. There were probably hundreds of Lius in the phone book and even more on central registries, but that didn't stop a crawling sensation at the base of Daremo's neck. Kao Fei was sending him to the right place; of this he was certain. He remembered the man's broken, squishy body beneath his fist and fingers, blood and information pouring from his ruined mouth.

Daremo had convinced him that he had been used, abused, and then abandoned by Liu Chia. He had done this by convincing Fei, in turn, that he wasn't an Interpol agent, that Liu Chia—supposedly a hireling—was using Fei as a front, as a diversion, as an expendable distraction to the Ninja Master.

He had convinced the drug warlord that he had been dishonored before death, a fate deemed horrible even by scum like Kao Fei. He was no longer duty bound to keep the *Moshuh Nanren's* secrets. In Fei's mind, at any rate, he was an honorable man. Drugs had an "honorable" tradition in China. They were brought in by the British, for heaven's sake, in 1800. The "foreign mud," as it was called, led to the opium wars, the Boxer Rebellion, and ultimately the People's Republic.

Kao Fei died with honor by essentially hiring a ninja to right the injustice done to him by Liu Chia. He begged his killer to seek out and punish the reason for his killing.

Daremo walked on, resisting the urge to stare at his hands, Lady Macbeth-like. What was all this guilt, regret, and longing doing up there? His mind was coming apart, he could feel it.

Whatever happened to it in San Francisco years ago; whatever had happened to it on the trip from Israel to Hong Kong, whatever was happening to it was catching up to Daremo. Everybody was playing with things they couldn't understand—only Daremo was playing the roles of both Dr. Frankenstein and the monster. He must have been experimenting on himself.

He couldn't feel before, and now he was feeling too much. It was getting in the way of his quest. Worse, it was making him question the quest. Why discover one's purpose? Why discover the *Moshuh Nanren*'s plot? He didn't have to. He had attained levels beyond that of most of the world's population. He had reached a level of personal accomplishment beyond most people's understanding. He was a consummate martial artist, in consummate physical shape. He could throw ice shards into people's heads, for heaven's sake!

And he had made his fortune. He had masterminded

a plan to rob an Iranian bank. The plan had no back doors, but it didn't need one. If he had not succeeded, he would not have wanted to escape. But they had pulled it off and now he was financially set for life. So why not screw the *Moshuh Nanren*, screw the ninja? If they wanted him, why not let them come after him? Why go to them?

He didn't know why—he couldn't begin to understand why—but he kept walking north. He walked until he reached the train station in Lo Wu, the border town.

The military and police were crawling all over the place. Their uniforms looked exactly the same, except for the colors and symbols. For some reason that Daremo didn't understand—he was getting pretty sick of not understanding why he understood—he knew which was which.

The police, otherwise known as the Public Security Bureau, wore the white and blue uniforms with the country's symbol on their caps. The blue and green uniforms with the same emblem marked the New Armed Security Force. Army men were there as well, wearing white and blue uniforms with a red star on their caps. The emblem symbol were their badges. Daremo could see people wearing the same kind of clothes, but he instinctively knew they weren't official because they had no emblems on their caps.

Entering Lo Wu was like crossing the line from a prosperous suburban community to an overtaxed urban area. The roadway instantly changes from smooth, thick asphalt to worn, crumbling asphalt. The change from Sheung Shui to here was just as pronounced. It wasn't so much the road but the entire environment. It became more severe, more ominous, more Orwellian.

Eyes were everywhere, and all were watching. Daremo stood, taking in the complex network of rail lines and the crush of official and unofficial Chinese bodies. To his surprise, his stress-rife brain also became more severe, more exacting. It was as if the boss came back from lunch and the goldbricking dreamers snapped back to attention. All the doubts were swept out and the spotlights were turned on.

People were looking at him, and not just out of passing curiosity or sidelong glances. There were people in the crowds looking directly at him. The police and militia continued to get people off the Kowloon/ Canton trains to check their visas and have them walk the three hundred meters to the connecting train, but out of those folk there were several who were paying particular attention to Daremo.

What good are you, Daremo complained to himself bitterly. Lo Wu was the main transfer point between Hong Kong and the People's Republic. The *Moshuh Nanren* knew enough about his coming to set Kao Fei on him. They would also know enough to have scouts at the border. As he watched, the figures started to make their nonchalant way toward him.

Daremo turned. He walked away from the people. He didn't want to kill anymore. He wanted to see if he could get to Liu Chia without having to kill anymore. He rationalized: that was the more difficult, the more impressive, wasn't it? That was exactly what the *Moshuh*

Nanren weren't expecting, wasn't it? Yeah sure, they'd be surprised; they'd be off balance.

Daremo joined the crowd of Caucasion and Oriental tourists milling around the train station. It was mid-morning. The air was brisk but clear. People felt refreshed, renewed. They paid almost no attention to the round-eye as he carefully maneuvered among them, keeping his lead on the people coming after him. He walked until he was amid the steam and electric engines of the trains.

He waited until he was in the thick of the main crowd outside a series of burnished green passenger cars. Daremo glanced back quickly, then pulled himself up onto the train. He slipped inside the car to his left, keeping an eye out for either the police or his followers.

To his amazement, the train was comfortable, almost luxurious—nothing at all like the chug he had come up the New Territories on. That had been the standard slow train. The trains came in three categories—special express, direct express, and slow. Within those categories came four classes within the vehicle's walls; soft sleeper, soft seat, hard sleeper, and hard seat. The difference was many HK dollars and several hours of shuteye.

But this was a train of a different color. Red, in fact. Red walnut paneling and red carpeting. Green velvet drapes. Brass door fixtures. This was the Imperial Peking Express, the Republic's first luxury train and a sweeping sign of the changes of the "Four Modernizations" period following the repressive Cultural Revolution.

Daremo chided himself. So much for finding a hiding place on this train. He doubted that any nook or cranny of this proud achievement would go unchecked before the final destination of Peking, or, as they termed it, Beijing. So much for stowing away onboard. Now he had to get off without facing the Em-en agents.

Damn the language anyway. It was what turned Peking into Beijing and Yenlo Wang into Yue Lan. They pronounced *c* as "ts," *q* as "ch," *x* as "sh," *z* as "ds," and *zh* as the initial "j." It is what is known as the Peking dialect, which only holds in Peking. Everyone everywhere else has his own Cantonese dialect.

If his mind wasn't feeding him translations, he'd be helpless. He only hoped he didn't wind up in some city where his mind went blank. Considering the way he felt, that could happen anytime. Daremo rushed through the narrow hall of the lushly appointed train and stepped out through the first exit he found. Again his mind picked out his adversaries—much closer now—freezing the entire tableau for a second.

He clearly saw one of them talking to a green-suited army man and pointing in his direction. That was it, then. He had been seen emerging from the Imperial Express. He was the brown-haired round-eye in black. Soon all the militia and police would be told of his suspicious actions. He doubted he would be shot on sight, but he would be stopped and asked for identification he didn't have.

Daremo entered the crowd again, moving back the way he had come, to the center of the station. The

Em-ens would work quickly. They would try to block all his exits and what they couldn't guard, they'd get the unknowing militia to do. He not only didn't want to kill, he couldn't afford to kill here. That would tighten the security all the more.

Any deaths here would probably be tied in with the Yue Lan fight of a few scant hours ago. That had been done by a round-eye in black as well. Even the provincial Chinese police couldn't miss the connection. Daremo didn't know what to do. He didn't want to retreat, but it looked like he had no choice. He had to fight through the army and Em-ens blocking his escape, then return to a less populated area of the frontier.

He had to hope he could sneak across the huge Chinese border like a wetback getting into California. The Great Wall of China only stretched four thousand miles from the Bohai Sea to the Gobi Desert. That was still a thousand miles to the north. It couldn't keep him out. But perhaps the *Moshuh Nanren* could keep him in. Everywhere he turned he saw the people his brain had warned him about.

He looked for a crowd of tourists he could meld with, but his mental state was unsure. He wasn't positive he could make himself invisible. And he couldn't risk not being sure. He needed help, an extra edge. He stopped walking among the sea of people between the trains and tried to calm his whirring brain.

He hadn't slept in more than a day. He hadn't eaten for that long as well. He was having an anxiety attack. He could feel it. He had to *use* it. He tried to forget his mortality and think like a ninja, like a cornered animal.

Daremo remembered the feeling. He remembered—or, more accurately, his mind showed him—a sequence of events: back in San Francisco, the same exhausted sensation of bravado that had led him to kill a mafia chieftain with a credit card and his lawyer with a sharpened car radio antenna.

Talk about insane. Daremo had been in the same emotional state then as he was now. And he had gotten away with it then, just as he was going to get away with changing clothes with a policeman now.

That's what he was going to do, all right. Take a policeman in a silencing, paralyzing grip into a bathroom, shove him in a stall, knock him out, and change clothes with him. Pull the cap low across his face, shorten himself by hunching over and using other ninja muscle tricks, then walk right through a militia-guarded entrance.

Now all he had to do was reach a policeman near a lav without any Em-ens around. His pausing on the platform didn't help matters much. The adversaries were closer now, closing in on four sides. He ignored their proximity, just kept moving toward the small station house, where people waited on line for tickets.

He felt certain that the Em-ens wouldn't have guns among their loose cloths or satchels. They couldn't risk being caught with them. Normally, there was little danger of that, but they were going up against a ninja. If they got close enough to shoot him without hitting an innocent bystander, they were close enough for him to throw off their aim or kill them. And if a gun went off here, the armed guards would swarm like an angry horde of hornets to shoot down the escaping assassin.

Daremo grinned as they drew closer. He saw a woman coming in from the left and a young man coming in from the right. They were dressed like traditional Chinese citizens. Behind him were an older man and woman. He wasn't going to depend on traditional thinking, that fighting the older man or woman might be easier. An older person could be a more experienced master of martial arts.

Daremo continued to move in the same direction. He would let them come to him. He was on an unavoidable collision course with the young man, which would have them meeting just outside the entrance to the station house. As they neared each other, the young man tripped. He dove forward, his arms out. His forefingers shot at Daremo's eye and throat.

People were jostled aside by the falling youth. Daremo pivoted to his right, catching the man's wrist in one hand and letting the fingers of his other hand curl in around the youth's wrist. Amazing: petrified tortoise style. Talk about obscure!

Daremo dodged the blows, got himself behind the falling man, and "broke" the youth's fall. He also broke the youth's back with a devastating kick. The kick was shielded from others' eyes by the youth's body. He arched his body, then collapsed. Again, Daremo's inner intensity had allowed him to deliver a devastating blow that merely looked like a step forward.

The kid was *Moshuh Nanren,* all right. He collapsed, only a wheezing sound escaping from between his teeth. His training would not allow him to cry out. But even without the shout, people began congregating around the fallen youth. On the crowded platform he was a noticeable obstruction, and the more people who tripped over him or called to him, the better.

Crowds begat crowds as more curious passersby went over to see what the fuss was about. That emptied the area Daremo was moving toward, but it also cleared the way for the young woman. The two older people were caught in the crowd.

Daremo got into the station house first, cursing himself. The kick had been instinctive. He had hardly had any control over it. His mind considered the situation and acted accordingly. Ah hell, maybe the kid wouldn't die. It was only a broken back, after all. He moved as quickly as he could without drawing attention to himself. But the young girl was as skilled and swift a mover as he.

As soon as she entered the station house, she called to him as if he were a friend. What was he going to do, ignore her? Not when the cop he wanted to reach remained at his post near the bathroom door. That was diagonally across the room from Daremo, who stood in the middle of the rectangular room. Along one wall were the ticket booths. Opposite, a few feet in front of the other wall, was a long bench. On either side were bathroom doors.

Better to face the girl at any rate. It was a big mistake to turn your back on an Em-en. Daremo looked at her and smiled, waiting for the move. It came almost immediately. She went to take his arm. One hand became a snake, the other a mantis pincer. The snake cleared the target. The pincer moved in to disrupt the kidneys, the spleen, and the intestines.

Daremo turned and took her in his arms. The pincer slid along his back. The snake was caught between their two bodies. He kissed her, his own fingers probing her neck. He held her under the arms and continued toward the bathroom.

The older couple had untangled themselves from the curious onlookers and came at Daremo's back. He waited until there was almost no room to retreat, then turned.

"Is this what you were looking for?" he asked in Cantonese, and gave them back the girl as if she were their daughter. Considering *Mushuh Nanren* ways, she could have been. The old woman had to hold on to the groggy girl to keep her from collapsing while the man came forward, his hand out in greeting. They couldn't let the girl collapse and blame Daremo. That would have meant reports and arrests and trials. They wanted Daremo dead, not jailed.

When the old man was close enough to the round-eye so Daremo's body blocked the cop's view, the outstretched vertical hand became horizontal and shot toward Daremo's sternum like a spear. Daremo knocked it aside and stepped in, embracing the older man. Their legs moved slightly, quickly. The man defeated Daremo's purpose of kneeing the Em-en's balls into his upper intestines.

They broke from their embrace. The old man tried to grab Daremo's hands, but they fluttered around the grasping fingers like birds. The old man instantly kicked forward. Daremo's knees locked around the man's ankle. He twisted as if falling to one knee. The old man was pushed to the side. To cover his backward stumbling, he moved over to a bench. The old man sat down heavily as Daremo continued his movement to sit down next to him.

Daremo motioned for the two women to join them. He did so pinioning the older man's arm with one hand and putting his elbow in the old man's throat. The Em-en's eyes clouded over. The woman sat the younger girl down next to the man and went to take a seat next to Daremo. She kept her eyes on him as she sat. He crossed his legs and she started, leaping up again.

The cop by the lav, which was behind them and to the left, looked curiously at that, a look the old woman could not ignore. She fluttered her hands as if saying, "It's nothing," and slowly sat down next to a widely smiling Daremo.

"*Her shiann tzay?*" he said. And now?

"*Way gwo goou,*" she answered quietly. Foreign dog. "You are doing exactly as we hoped."

"That is why you're trying to kill me?" Daremo asked pleasantly with a disbelieving smile.

"We are not trying to kill you. We are trying to warn you," the woman maintained angrily. "We only defend ourselves from your attack."

"Like on Yue Lan," Daremo suggested sarcastically.

"The drug pushers would have you dead because their aims do not match ours."

Daremo ignored the ramifications of the statement. "Which are?"

"A better world."

Daremo giggled.

"You are doing exactly what the ninja want you to. You will kill yourself fighting us when you should be fighting them!"

"Give me time," he suggested. "Tell me more."

The woman picked up her satchel from the floor and started rummaging through it. "You shall see," she said.

"You won't," he said as the blade came through the side of the bag. In one motion he stood up, one hand on her cheek as if caressing her face. Instead, his finger curled under her jawbone and dislocated it in such a way that the blood to her brain was cut off. The blade went into the old man's side.

Both her hands had been inside the bag. She had made herself vulnerable, hoping her words would keep Daremo from acting until she could get the knife— poisoned, no doubt—into him. With a powerfully controlled push, he brought the old couple together, pushing the blade all the way into the old man's guts.

"Thanks very much," he told them as he moved to stand before the groggy girl. "Have a nice day." He put his hand on her neck and leaned down to suggest she stay with her folks awhile. As he did so, he pushed her Adam's apple to her spinal cord with his thumb.

So much for the moratorium on killing.

Daremo smiled and smiled and smiled. That was three, maybe four, more on his conscience. He'd definitely have to go on a temple pilgrimage when he got back to Japan to pray for their souls.

Hao shyh, he thought. Good try. He didn't believe the woman for a second. Sure, the ninja were trying to kill him, but the *Moshuh Nanren* weren't just defending themselves . . . were they?

Daremo remembered his confrontations with the Figure in Black. He remembered how the Figure almost always instigated the attacks, but he also remembered instances when he himself was at a disadvantage the Figure did not take advantage of.

Daremo actually shook his head. The cop in front of the lav door took it as confusion. Daremo was really clearing his mind of the doubts. The doubts changed nothing, he decided. The mind weapons were still too dangerous and had to be destroyed. Liu Chia, the Figure in Black, had the weapons, so Daremo had to confront the Figure.

But he had to get into the People's Republic of China first. And to do that he had to get out of the Lo Wu train station. And he was ready to do just that. His hands were itching for more blood. To heck with the idea of knocking out the cop. Kill the sucker. Why not? If he's dead, he won't be missed for a lot longer. If unconscious, he'd soon wake up and report. Yeah, kill the miserable son of a bitch.

Daremo walked up to the cop, smiling widely. The cop's expression was attentive, concerned, helpful. The ninja opened his mouth as if to ask a question. He started to raise his arms, his finger bent into the shape of claws.

A hand fell on Daremo's shoulder from behind. He whirled around. He stared into the face of the Monkey King.

10

The Monkey King was in China. And Daremo was the Monkey King.

He had turned to face the same cartoon monkey martial artist who had performed onstage during the Yue Lan celebration. He brought the Occidental to the same blustering, bearded figure that had helped him at the end of the performance. In fact, the entire Peking Opera troupe of a dozen people were in the railway station, preparing to enter the People's Republic, their booking in Kowloon having been completed.

They were all still in makeup and costume, entertaining the travelers like members of an American carnival. They all congregated around their four trucks. As they milled around, preparing to leave, the director, in his guise as a bearded soldier, took Daremo aside.

"You are in trouble, are you not?" he asked quietly.

Daremo nodded. "I can understand that," the bearded man in the heavy makeup said. "I saw what happened at the Shaukiwan Temple. Come, come with me."

When the military checked on the troupe's papers, they found thirteen members. All were in heavy character makeup and ornate costume, save one. He wore a mask of the Monkey King—the most famous and beloved character in the canon—and his clothes were a simple, baggy blue tunic and pants. He had slippers on his feet and held a straight staff in his hand.

The policeman in charge slowly surveyed the group. He walked all the way down the line, until he reached the man in the Monkey King mask. And then slowly, purposefully, he reached up and pulled the mask off.

The Monkey King made a face, pulled the cop's hat off, fell to his knees, and crawled through the policeman's legs. The military men laughed in appreciation. The policeman whirled, yelling, until he saw the athletic antics of the actor, who twirled on one hand, catapulted to his feet, and danced around on bent knees like a drunken Russian.

Finally, the policeman too laughed, strode over and pulled his cap from the Monkey King's hands with mock anger. To be honest, he really wasn't expecting anything unusual or ominous. It just struck him as strange that the man at the end of the line would have a mask while the others wore makeup. He realized that it was a trick to take him in. The makeup that was beneath was exactly the same as the mask, exactly the kind of trick the Monkey King would play.

He let the troupe pack in and drive off after inquiring

where they would be performing next. His vaunted parents and in-laws would enjoy seeing a company like this. It was small, but the members were obviously talented and imaginative. The leader of the group told him their next performance would be in the village of Ganzhou in the state of Jiangxi, some two hundred miles away.

It might very well be worth it. Buddha knew the paper work concerning the injured young man on the platform would be exhausting. Imagine, a simple fall like that causing a broken back. Ah, well. Two hundred miles was a long way, but he could use the refreshing break from the cinemas. That's all his kids wanted to do—wear jeans and sneakers and go to the cinema. Perhaps they needed a reeducation on the fine art of ancient Chinese theater.

Daremo thanked the bearded one and prepared to leave the moving truck. His savior sat in the rear of the vehicle, in the covered flatbed. Another man, an actor, was up front in the cab, driving. The inside was lit from sunlight outside. It was decorated with hanging curtains and tapestries, which rocked like fans as the wheels maneuvered on the roads. There was a bed attached to one wall and a chair and table attached to the wall separating the cab from the flatbed.

He did not ask why the man, had saved him. He didn't really want to know. It could have been a *Moshuh Nanren* subterfuge, but it hardly made sense in that light. Even if what the old woman had said was true— that the *Moshuh Nanren* were just defending them- selves from a renegade ninja—why save him and bring him on Chinese soil? In any case, it was best to take off when the taking off was good.

"Please sit," the man requested, holding his arm out toward the bed. Daremo figured he owed him that much. If he tried to kill the round-eye, then at least Daremo would know for sure that this was just another Em-en subterfuge.

Even beyond that, there was something about this bearded man's face and tone that piqued Daremo's curiousity. He came back and sat down on the bed several feet from the man. The bed was just a mattress on legs, so the ninja could see clearly that no one and nothing was lying beneath.

The bearded man made several false starts. He obviously found what he was going to say very difficult. Daremo watched him carefully, trying to see through the makeup.

The hair on the man's head, under the headdress he had taken off, was his own. It was black, with some white streaks through it. His face was round and wide, with a few extra pounds of fat. The eyes were dark brown. As soon as the headdress had come off, he had put glasses on the end of his nose.

"Please forgive my presumption," he said in his Cantonese dialect, "but I must ask." He leaned in, his brows coming together, deep lines appearing on his forehead. "This trouble you are in. Has it anything to do with . . . drugs?"

Daremo watched him carefully, using all the talents at his disposal to "read" the man. Everything he felt, saw, and heard seemed to indicate that he was not *Moshuh Nanren.*

"How did you know?" he finally replied.

The bearded man leaned back, looking toward the ceiling, clapping his hands and shaking his head. "I knew it, it had to be," he said tiredly, "Are you . . . you are not a drug seller, are you?"

Daremo shook his head. "I did not think so," the man said. "It made no sense otherwise."

"What didn't make sense?" Daremo pressed. "How did you know it was drugs?"

"Please excuse me," the man said, leaning back toward Daremo. "If you had been a drug pusher, they would have never attacked you the way they did that night in the temple. A bullet or bomb would have been your fate. As an Interpol or police agent, they could have made your death seem a regrettable Yue Lan accident . . . a confused white man accidentally being stabbed or burned during the celebration."

Okie-dokie, Daremo thought. It made a certain thin sense taken out of context.

"I knew it had to be drug-related," the man continued, "because they would not have gone to such trouble to kill you otherwise. Again, they would have shot you or planted a bomb in your car. But that would have alerted the police, who would have no option but to crack down, bribes or no bribes."

The man was spinning a theory more to the wall than to Daremo. But after he voiced his reasoning, he returned his attention to the man. "You are an exceptional martial artist."

"You're not so bad yourself," Daremo answered. "Who are you?"

"Please excuse my rudeness," the bearded one said. They were big on "please excusing." "Please call me Zhang Meng. I am Zhang Meng."

"Well, thank you again Mr. Zhang. "Daremo got up again, having used the correct terminology. The first name was the Family name in China.

Meng stood alongside. "Please." This time the word was pleading. "Will you not stay with the tour? It is safer that way."

Daremo looked at him with total distrust. This make no sense at all. "Please pardon me, Mr. Zhang," he said, putting the "excuse me" shoe on the other foot. "I owe you a service, but I cannot understand why you wish my humble company." Now that wasn't too bad. He could speak twisted politese with the best of them. "Why are you so concerned with my safety?"

"I could see you were being pursued at the train station," the man said quickly. "The danger for you is not over. I . . . I lost my family to the drug trade." He sat down in his seat heavily, looking at the floor.

Now, wait a minute. All the *Moshuh Nanren* had seemed dedicated to do since Daremo arrived was kill him. Twice they almost cornered him and twice this Peking Opera director helps him out. Okay, given that extremely suspicious behavior, let's say Zhang Meng *was* an Em-en.

What the hell for? What the hell was he doing? Trying to gain Daremo's trust. For what? To take him into China, become his trusted friend, and then kill him? Where's the logic in that? Okay, maybe the *Moshuh Nanren* think the only way they could get close enough to kill him is to get under his defenses. And maybe the way to get under his defenses is to become his trusted friend.

But *nobody* was going to become Daremo's trusted friend. He would never let anybody become his trusted. friend. He had let his guard down for Michelle Bowers, sure, but that was different. And he had certainly learned his lesson there. He wasn't going to sleep with Zhang Meng. And he wasn't going to sleep with any of Meng's female troupe either. Have sex, maybe, but never let his defenses down.

And if Zhang Meng was an Em-en, he'd *know* that. He'd know there was no chance of becoming Daremo's buddy. Fine, then Zhang might very well be on the level. Besides, Daremo had to get farther up north and there were few things as noticeable as a paleface round-eye loping through town. All right, then, enough logic. Back to the story.

"Perhaps you have wondered why you have never seen my face," Meng was continuing, looking up at Daremo, his painted visage haunted. "My wife . . . and children . . . were killed by criminals. I . . . killed the murderers myself . . . with my bare hands. I am a fugitive."

Time out. What a story. But if it could happen to Daremo's "great grandfather," Brian Williams, it was tenuously possible that it had happened to Zhang Meng. And no Em-en, no matter how bold, would use a copycat story like that to achieve sympathy.

But even if it was all bullshit and the entire troupe

were Em-en killers, then Daremo had found what he was looking for. They would either kill him or take him to the Figure in Black.

"I would be honored to assist you in any way I can," said Zhang Meng, falling to his knees, bowing his head, and holding out his clenched hands in supplication.

Daremo took his arms and brought him to his feet. "It is I who owe you the service," he reminded him. "What can I do for you?"

As it turned out, the group was happy to have an extra member. Since the advent of movies—an art form the Chinese only became proficient at in the late seventies—the Peking Opera troupes had fallen on tough times. There were still plenty of places to perform, but the big money was in the cities and the cities were becoming the property of cinemas.

The young men and women who flocked to the urban centers to find jobs were losing interest in the ancient theatrical arts, and the opera's biggest fans were dying of old age in droves. The troupes had to cut back members and expenses. But for the better of the groups, beautiful costumes and props were still a must. That, and the skills of the martial artist actors, is what kept a company going.

"What you saw performed on the night of Yue Lan is called 'Havoc In Heaven,'" Meng told him when they stopped in Conghua for something to eat. The rural lifestyle in China was completely different than Hong Kong. Even in a country of over a billion people, the villages had an unpopulated, unhurried look to them. The absence of people, on the streets, he was assured, was due to everyone working all day. They left their *pingtangs* (flathouses) early in the morning to grow rice or do construction or repair work. The children had to be in school or in the fields. The mothers had either to tend the garden or laboriously shop for food, standing in long lines for each item. It was worse in the cities but no great shakes in the country, either.

The trucks were pulled over to the side of the road and several girls and one boy pulled out three cinder blocks and a large wok from the back of the truck. They set the cinder blocks up in a C pattern and lay the steel bowl on it. In the open side of the C they placed twigs and firewood. They had the "stove" going in a couple of minutes. In the wok they made millet rice and chicken.

The troupe members sat in a circle, each with his own bowl, shoveling the food into their mouths with chopsticks. Daremo sat beside Zhang, doing exactly the same thing. He was introduced around by Meng, still in his makeup. Daremo too still had the vestiges of the Monkey King on his face, but both men were wearing light blue street clothes.

"We didn't do all of it," said Yuen Baio, the young chef with sparkling eyes, long face, and crooked teeth. "Just the most exciting part."

"The cinema's excitement requires that we do all the 'good' parts almost right away," said Fu Liang, another young man.

"It's a story taken from a famous novel called 'Journey to the West,' " Meng continued. "The Monkey King 'Sun Wukong' has obtained a magic weapon for the Dragon King of the East Sea. With it, he creates all sorts of mischief. He disrupts the Queen Mother of Heaven's peach banquet..."

"Eating all the peaches save one," laughed Shih Miao, a girl with a cleft chin, long, narrow eyes, straight nose, and a beautiful smile.

"He drinks the wine of immortality and leaves heaven by the South Gate," Meng further related. "On the way home to his Mountain of Flowers and Fruit, he must battle the soldiers of the Jade Emperor."

"That's what I saw," Daremo remembered.

"And that's who I was," said Meng, slapping himself on the chest. "A jade Emperor soldier."

"And I was the Monkey King!" Fu Liang trumpeted, much to the dismay of the others. "Until now," he finished miserably.

Daremo noted that these performers lived their lives broadly, even off the stage. "Don't worry, Mr. Fu," he said. "It's just a mask."

"Like mine," said Zhang Meng sternly to the others. "Mr. Mo is my assistant and must be accorded the same respect I receive." He looked at Daremo. "And he is Liang to you. They do not deserve the respect of Mister." The troupe was chastised and subdued. "Yet," he told them, brightening the mood considerably.

They packed up their things and returned to the road. Zhang needed the time to confer with Daremo. "We cannot hope to compete with the funded state opera," he said as the truck continued northward. "We cannot put on the grand battle scenes of the city companies. We must be content with intimate performances of a few people. We concentrate on the delicate details of our performance—the singing, the pantomine, the dialogue, and the acrobatics."

Each was specifically and exactingly combined in Peking Opera. It was almost like human animation. In cartoon animation, the character is given life in twenty-four individual drawings for each second of movement. The opera was not as severe, but close. Every action was directed specifically, every muscle coordinated, including the facial and vocal muscles.

"Tomorrow night we will perform 'Autumn River' in Ganzhou," Meng decided. "Followed by 'Stealing Silver' and 'At the Crossroads.' That's always a favorite." He sighed and leaned back. "I remember the days when the performances lasted five, six hours." He leaned forward again, writing in a small, stapled notebook. "Now we're lucky if we can keep them awake for two."

"Bored?" Daremo inquired reluctantly. He hated playing straight man.

"Dying," said Meng. "These days we're blessed if any of our audience is under seventy years of age."

While Meng busied himself with business, Daremo spent most of the day watching China go by from the back of the truck. Although he was tempted to spend some time in the cab with Li Lianjie, the driver, and Hung Donglian, the other girl of the troupe, a taller than usual girl with a long neck, wide nose, and thin lips, he thought it best to keep interaction to a minimum.

Southeast China was subtropical, thanks to the lower Yangtze River and its many tributaries. Although the view was often locked in with trees and leafy foilage, the fauna occasionally broke for impressive views of rich green and red river basins and light sparkling brown water—reflecting the color of the riverbeds.

At one point Daremo heard a rustling roar from above and watched gleefully as they passed a "flying waterfall," in which nature had deemed to create a strange shaped cliff topped with a river. The water cascaded down in glorious patterns across the stone and leaves.

"'As if the Milky Way were pouring from the sky,'" Meng wistfully quoted. "From a poem by the famous Tang Dynasty poet Li Bai," he said when Daremo looked at him.

When it grew dark and the sun reflected off the rich cumulonimbus clouds, bathing the entire area in deep orange, Meng lit a candle. The holder was securely attached to the tiny table next to the chair. As the truck lumbered into the night, Zhang told Daremo stories. He sat in the pale flickering yellow light and told his comrade about the Peking Opera.

"I imagine the action is very mannered and the music very nasty to you," he said. "But even that comes from ancient traditions. The garish colors were necessary, for in the days of the teahouse theaters, the stage was lit by oil lamps. We needed highly contrasting colors. And we needed loud instruments to attract an audience. But those audiences were uniformly rude. We needed specific actions to signify specific emotions so everything could be understood without hearing."

"Uh-huh," Daremo agreed. "How did you become a performer?"

Meng shrugged. "What choice did I have? I was a martial artist and a wanted murderer. What else could I do? Where else could I go where I wouldn't starve or be discovered?"

"How many years has it been?"

"Oh, I don't know. Perhaps eight, maybe more."

"Eight?" Daremo said in surprise. "Wouldn't the statute of limitations be up?"

"Statute?" Meng said in confusion. "I wouldn't know. And I certainly am not going to find out."

Irritated by his Western thinking, Daremo changed the subject. "The makeup is a nice touch."

"I got the idea from your James Stewart...in a movie entitled *The Greatest Show on Earth*."

"Where he dressed up as a clown," Daremo remembered, laughing at the incongruity.

"Correct. We have our clowns, too. They are called *chou*. They can be recognized by a patch of white paint around the eyes and nose. I usually do not play the *chou*. My roles, as you have seen, are the *jing*, the 'painted faces' roles—the soldiers, the generals, the demons, and so forth."

"Something for everyone."

"Exactly. The *sheng*, *jing*, and *chou* are all male roles of many different types and subdivisions. The *dan* are female roles, also with many subcategories. It used to be that men would play all the roles, *dan* or no. Thankfully, that has changed. It is a pleasure to have a woman's touch and company."

Daremo could not agree. He thought of Michelle, but her image was cloudy, indistinct. It had somehow combined with all the faces of his loved ones. He saw Rhea—her beautiful Japanese face infused with frustrated desire and tortured concern. He saw Rachel Assaf's face—at first soft, lovesick, desperate, then cold, distant. Finally, he remembered her as he had seen her last, her expression of need turning to horror.

Their faces melted away. Daremo started to turn mentally from the images, but something attracted his attention. When he looked back, there were other faces—faces he could not recognize. They were faces he knew—from somewhere—but did not know exactly.

It was more than perplexing. It was alarming. Their images set off buried emotions inside him. They touched off his internal alarms. His angelic self was leaping on his right shoulder, pointing at them and screeching. One face was Oriental, but different from Rhea's. It was also beautiful, but serene . . . unnaturally serene. The last one was plain and round, with short brown hair and hazel eyes.

It was the most disturbing image, because it had no expression at all.

"*Wei. Lao pengyou, wei!*"

He heard the words as if from a distance at first. Then his eyes cleared and he could see Meng leaning over him, talking. It took several more seconds for his mind to pump up the translations. "Hello, are you there? Old friend, are you there?"

"Yes," he replied uncertainly. "I'm all right."

"Are you tired? Would you like to rest?"

"No, that's all right," Daremo said vacantly. "I'm fine."

Meng needed further assurance and got it. He finally empathized, admitting that he often remembered his murdered wife in the same way. "Come," he suggested. "We have stopped for the night."

They went outside to find the town of Meixian, near the southern borders of both Jiangxi and Fujian on the east China coast. Yuen had been sent off with some money to buy some treats, and Shih tended the cooking rice.

"Not Baio!" Meng wailed, clutching the sides of his head. When the young man had returned, Daremo understood Zhang's reaction. Yuen had spent most of the money on dessert. There was *Chien tsang goe* (thousand layer cake), *ma tai goe* (fried water chestnut sticks), and *daan tats* (egg custard tarts). Even the buns he bought were sweet: *lin yung bau* (mashed lotus seed bun) and the tempting *shiu tsing gou* (sweet fungus dumpling).

Even with the humbling name, Daremo enjoyed the *shiu tsing gou* most of all. It was like flavorful mushrooms inside pastry. He ate while Meng chased Baio around the fire with the Monkey King's stick.

"All right, all right!" the young man cried, reaching under his loose jacket for two more bags, out of which he threw more dumplings and buns at everyone. These were the *shiu mai* (steamed meat dumpling) and *ngau yuk bau* (fried beef bun).

"You've wiped us out!" Zhan moaned in mock despair. "We're bankrupt, paupers!" He renewed his chase as Baio ran, dove, flipped, and somersaulted around the fire.

Then he made the mistake of leaping over a sitting Daremo. Suddenly the round-eye was up, a hand wrapped around each of Baio's wrists. With a snap, he spun the diving Yuen over and onto his feet. He held him in place around the waist so the momentum wouldn't topple Baio over. Then, as Meng charged him, Daremo catapulted himself over Yuen in an upside-down handstand on the boy's shoulders. He landed in front of the lad as the stick came down on Baio's head.

Yuen groaned in mock pain, clutching his skull as the others laughed, oohed, and aahed. "I've seen him in action," Meng told them, referring to Daremo. "Now you you know why I made him a member of the troupe." Soon everyone was on their feet and around the round-eye.

"I know a little something about shadow boxing," he answered their questions. "And a little weapons work."

"Do you know the double rings?" Fu Liang asked.

"Or the double hooks?" inquired Cheung Chen.

"I know sword-and-knife play mostly," Daremo admitted.

"Not the spear, not the scimitar?" Hung Donglian pressed.

"Enough!" Meng shouted. Instant silence. "Is this the way you treat a *tongzhi*? Is this the way you would treat me? How dare you speak to my associate in that fashion!" The group was again severely chastised by Zhang's angry tone and justifiable disappointment.

"Just for that," he said, grinning at Daremo, "you must suffer through a demonstration of our skills."

The troupe looked up in surprised pleasure, but

quickly returned to their subjugated frown, lest they incur the wrath of their director again.

"Please, sir," said Li Lianjie. "Do not concern yourself with such distracting punishment."

"Silence, pup!" Meng bellowed, hitting him on the head with the Monkey King's stick. Then, in rapid succession, he hit him on the shoulder, elbow, stomach, knee, shin, and foot. The boy responded to each blow in a different exaggerated position, making the others work hard to keep from laughing.

"The student's actions are the master's actions," Meng declared. "To reprimand you, I must reprimand myself!" He looked at Daremo for corroboration. The ninja nodded. "Very well," said the director. He threw the stick to Daremo, who caught it.

From the back of a truck, Zhang took what looked like a black and white basketball attached to a stick. It was the weapon he knew Daremo had seen him use onstage during the "Havoc in Heaven" performance. When he charged Daremo now, they recreated the battle the round-eye had witnessed at the Yue Lan festival.

The ninja's brain recalled the scene, even though he had only seen parts of it with peripheral vision. Then the new, improved mind studied the Monkey King's movements, translated them in Draemo's terms, and sent messages out along his nerves to his muscles. What the eyes didn't see was improvised by Daremo, who utilized the precepts the other movements taught him.

It was the mark of a great martial artist: It took more

than knowledge of one's own skill. It took recognition and analysis of the opponent's skill. It took strategy and conceptual thinking to almost instantly devise a defense and counterattack that played on the enemy's limitations. And all this had to be done withing the first few seconds of the fight.

The men tested each other's skills until the rest of the group watched with dropped jaws as the opponents' speed and dexterity became almost blinding and nearly unbelievable. They danced together, as if each man was being controlled by the same mind. They were going too fast, and the technique was too dazzling, for anyone to believe that it hadn't been choreographed earlier.

Finally, the Monkey King triumphed, as the Monkey King always did. Daremo slipped the thin end of the staff between Meng's fingers and the ball handle as Zhang was executing a weapon-spin, then threw the ball from the bearded one's hand. Zhang stepped back, his arms wide and his mouth open in pseudo-surprise— all but admitting his theatrical defeat.

Then Daremo stepped back and suddenly executed the Monkey King's pose of triumph perfectly. The troupe applauded spontaneously, astonished at the American's abilities. They had never seen a white man that good. By the time he and Zhang returned to their truck, Mr. Mo had been completely accepted by the others—even the reluctant Liang.

"They're good kids," Meng said, sitting down in his chair. "I found them on the streets of the major cities— Nanning, Guangzhou, Guiyang, Changsha. They were students or beggers. When they had parents, the old people couldn't feed them often as not. But they were natural athletes and willing to learn."

Daremo couldn't believe it. The Chinese government subsidized their athletes. "Quite a sob story," he said, standing near the back opening.

Meng looked up and smiled, almost as if he could read Daremo's mind. "Every word is true," he promised. "China has so many people, so many athletes. Many get lost in the passing flood."

Hm, Daremo thought. Maybe he *could* read my mind. "Maybe so," he said to the bearded one cryptically.

Zhang nodded toward the bed. "Tomorrow we enter Jiangxi," he said. "You'll need the rest."

Daremo looked toward the bed and then back at Meng. "I wouldn't think of it," he said. Then, to take the sting out of what could be considered an insult to a Chinese, he added, "I owe you so much already."

"I would be honored," Meng maintained.

"And I would be shamed. Please allow me to sleep outside, under the stars. The night is not bitter."

Zhang leaned back, surveyed Daremo, then nodded, smiling. "White man speak with silver tongue," he said, humorously paraphrasing another American movie he had seen.

Daremo laughed. "Roy Rogers," he guessed.

"Hiyo, Silver," Meng corrected. Then he motioned to the great outdoors. "Please."

Daremo hopped down from the truck, taking a padded blanket Zhang wouldn't let him leave without. He found a grassy section off the side of the road among a bed of pine needles. He lay on his back, looking up at the stars.

They did not change, wherever he was. There were always the stars and the inherent promise they gave: the promise of something else. No matter how ridiculous and horrible it became on earth, there was always... something else. Maybe more ridiculous, maybe more horrible, but still... something else.

Daremo thought about who he was and what he had done—and he didn't think about who he was and what he had done. The mental images just rolled around without his calling or bidding. Instead, he thought about the big, stupid things people under the stars and at the beach often thought about.

Life.

Birth.

Death.

Daremo looked at the stars and felt better than he ever had. He thought about birth and death and he came up with one "big" stupid conclusion.

I came from somewhere and I'm going somewhere.

Daremo fell alseep for the second to last time.

11

The universe was an egg.

Pangu was born a giant with a giant ax.

With the ax he split the egg. The white of the egg rose and became the sky. The yolk sank and became the earth.

Pangu saw what he had done and was afraid. He was afraid the two elements would merge again to recreate the dark chaos into which he had been born.

He place his hands upon the sky and his feet upon the earth. He grew one hundred and twenty inches each day, pushing the sky and the planet apart. He grew for thousands of years until he stood like a pillar between the ground and the atmosphere.

The world took form and solidified. The sky became firm and separate. Pangu stepped from between the orb and the air, then fell into a deep sleep.

His left eye turned into the sun.

His right eye turned into the moon.

His sweat turned into the dew.

The hairs on his body turned into the trees and flowers.

The parasites that lived in his flesh turned into the animals.

His body turned into mountains.

His blood turned into flowing rivers.

His bones turned into minerals.

His voice turned into thunder.

His breath turned into the wind and clouds.

That was how the world was created, she told him.

She was beautiful, naturally. But she was more than a woman. She was a god. She was Guanyin, the goddess of mercy.

"Why have you brought me here?" he asked her, drinking in her ethereal beauty. Specific points of beauty are somehow lost when faced with an angelic god. Considerations like eyes, nose, mouth, shape of head, hair, breasts, waist, derriere, and legs are ignored in the spirit state. She was Oriental, but even racial considerations like that lost their meaning in dreams.

She seemed confused by the question. Why ask, why answer, questions? Don't question, accept. But she was the goddess of mercy. She answered simply.

"I . . . look down upon the world and . . . hear its cries."

They walked together through the Chinese heaven. He loved it all but was confused by the languid environment. They passed dozens of others in a slow walk, but never so close that Daremo could distinquish their features. They were all distant, indistinct. But instinctively Daremo knew who they were. They passed door gods, they passed the thunder, lightning, and wind god. They passed gods of every kind.

Suddenly, Guanyin stopped before three figures. They stood directly in front of Daremo. They were as real as any person he had ever met. There were two seated men. One was bald, with long ears, a fleshy face, a large belly, and an eternal smile. The other was thin, with a long beard and moustache, which hung to his stomach. He, too, had a ready smile.

The female was the most impressive. She had the face of a woman but the teeth of a tiger and the tail of a leopard. Guanyin did not leave Daremo there. She held his arm and stood close by his side, almost protectively.

"This is Siddhartha Gautama," she said, holding her hand toward the bald man. "This is K'ung-fu-tzu," she introduced the next.

"I am the queen mother of the west," said the third. "They thought I should be here," she said of the other two. Daremo bowed his head in greeting. What do you say at times like this?

"Has she been telling you the Pangu story again?" the bald one asked with mirth. When Daremo nodded, he leaned toward the bearded one. "I should tell him about the five fingers, then," he quipped.

K'ung smiled and shook his head humbly. "It is also said that my five fingers made up the earth, air, fire, water, and wood," he said, holding up his hand. "And," he added, "that they also created a prison for the Mon-key King."

"They say much," the woman/beast interjected. "They say that dragons create invisible lines on the earth, that these lines are the dragon's veins and that to obstruct the lines means certain disaster. Who knows? They could be right."

"They say much," the Siddhartha agreed sadly. "Look what they have done with my words."

All three bowed their heads and considered their situation.

"The truth is..." came a bellowing voice behind them. Daremo turned to face a robust, muscular man with a high forehead and rich, long beard. He carried a long pole with a broad scimitar on the end. "The truth is that they have no place for us anymore, any of us. The truth of our wisdom only gets in their way."

Daremo looked at Guanyin. "Lord Guan," she introduced, "god of martial arts."

Daremo looked back at him in surprise. Lord Guan winked at him.

"No one invited you here," the queen mother snapped at the bare-chested deity.

"I have as much stake in this man as you," he countered with bold good humor.

"Perhaps more. Besides, I thought he might need an interpretor to understand your obtuse rhetoric."

"Our wisdom is no different than yours," K'ung said softly. "Only quieter."

Guan laughed. "Point taken, old man. And agreed."

That done, the group got down to business. The

Siddhartha sighed. "The first noble truth is that man's existence is *dukkha*."

"Full of suffering," Guanyin told Daremo, still at his arm.

"Full of conflict, dissatisfaction, and sorrow," the bald one elaborated. "The second noble truth is that all this is caused by man's selfish *tanha*.

"Desire," said Guanyin.

"Thirst," said Lord Guan. He said it as if he knew what it meant intimately.

The bald one closed his eyes. When he opened them again, he continued. "The third noble truth is that there is emancipation, liberation, and freedom from all this."

"Death?" Daremo asked, dreading it.

"*Jen*," said the bearded one.

"Love of man," Guanyin translated. "Love of life."

"Taken simply," said Lord Guan. "The Golden Rule." The martial arts god leaned toward the others. "It would work, too, if people were perfect, not flawed. But there's no getting around that. I've told you time and again."

"With art and nature blended harmoniously," the bearded one countered, "the superiour man feels neither anxiety nor fear... is always calm and at ease." He looked directly at Daremo with sympathetic eyes. "The inferior man is always worried and full of distress."

"Don't look now," said Lord Guan, "but I think you've just been insulted."

Daremo looked at all of them helplessly. "I am

distresed," he stammered, "because I do not understand what is happening me."

"To hear much," said K'ung, "select what is good and
follow it. See much and take careful note of it. These
are the steps by which one ascends to understanding."

"Ascends?" Daremo echoed.

"No doubt there are those who find it possible to act
without first understanding the situation," said K'ung,
"but I am not one of them."

"He has no choice!" Guan said angrily on Daremo's
behalf. "He must set things right."

"To govern is to set things right," K'ung replied
calmly. "If you begin by setting yourself right, who will
dare deviate from the right?"

Daremo heard other words in his brain. He heard
the words of the Central American shaman: "Seek not
survival but perfection." He remembered the old man's
tale of the seven stages of man, seven stages of earth.
He remembered it all but could not make heads or tails
of it. These were just words. If he did more than accept
them—if he tried to truly understand them—he would
go mad.

And that wasn't a very good idea for someone already
ki-chigaino. If he lost control now, when his mind was
more than human, he might unleash . . . well, something he had no control over.

"Tao is accepting and yielding," the queen mother
said suddenly, soothing his tortured thoughts. "Accept
and yield." She surveyed him as kindly as a woman
with tiger teeth and leopard tail could. "You will master
the laws of nature," she promised. "You will climb the

Moshuh Shan. You will ascend to understanding. Taoist magic can only be performed by a man of pure heart who is without evil."

Lord Guan put his arm around Daremo's shoulder. He smiled down at the mortal like a proud father.

"All is impermanent," said the Siddhartha. "All is floating reality."

"Life is just a short phase in the life of the soul," K'ung promised. "Life is but a fleeting moment compared to the slow change of the universe."

Daremo didn't like the sound of that. It sounded like the big kiss-off. It sounded like the promises of a trusted father to a dying son. Don't worry, Billy, there really *is* a heaven.

Daremo felt something. He felt something at his stomach. He looked down slowly, dreading the sight. There were three holes in his stomach. His legs were covered in blood.

I'm dead.

Not yet.

Soon?

Any second now.

Why?

You'll see.

When?

Any second now.

Don't you realize you're being used?" Guanyin asked in anguish. Siddhartha, K'ung, and the queen mother were gone.

Daremo looked down into her desperately caring face, remembering the others—the women he had left, the ones who had left him. When he looked into that face, the one seemingly so intent on saving him, he became angry.

"No I don't!" he replied. "Why don't you ever come right out and say things! Daremo, you're going to be attacked on the night of Yue Lan! You're going to climb Mount Huang to face the Figure in Black, Daremo. Why not just tell me? Why all this mystical crap?"

Lord Guan spun him around. "What do you think we are? Mindreaders? You think we can tell the future? Face up to it, We're only extensions of your subconscious. Whatever you don't want to deal with, you attribute to us. You've been using us as an excuse for years!"

"Excuse?" said the confused Daremo. "Excuse for what?"

Lord Guan grimaced. "By the name of my father, you have no patience. Just accept."

I'm dead.
Not yet.
I'm dead.
Hold on.
I can't.
Concentrate.
He looked down at his ruined middle. He felt the bullets grinding inside. He whined pathetically.
I can't.
Yes you can.
The dream fell apart because I can't think straight! I'm losing it!
You're not gone yet. You're still fighting.

I can't, I can't.

You must. For me.

W-w-w . . . what?

For me. You can't die yet. You must hold on for a few seconds more. Concentrate.

For me?

For me.

He used it as his mantra. To concentrate. To hold on for a few seconds more. For a few seconds, so he could understand.

For me.

For me.

For me.

Daremo awoke. He was losing his mind. He had experienced the dream at first as if it had been real, only to lose it at the end. Guanyin had tried to warn him of something. Or maybe he had used her, as Lord Guan had said, to reveal something to his conscious mind—something he should know, something he was overlooking.

But it was all gone now. All he had left now was a "real" world that didn't look the same, and Earth that had no real meaning anymore, a planet that had taken on the same validity as his dream heavens.

Ninja: no place on earth and none in heaven. Did the ninja leave them, or did they leave the ninja?

Was this it? Was Daremo going mad . . . or was he returning from *ki-chigaino* to sanity? Both were equally horrid fates.

Daremo spent the next day as a zombie. He walked

through the experiences like a robot keeping up only the most minimal of social responsibilities. He took on his role as Mr. Mo of this Peking Opera troupe so none of the actors became too friendly. Even Zhang Meng seemed to understand. He too fell into depressions.

The only thing that touched him in the next twenty-four hours was the actual performance in Ganzhou. It took place on an open-air stage in a temple courtyard. The night was beautiful, the surroundings were peaceful, and the audience full and appreciative.

But what Daremo appreciated most was the delicacy of the stories and the elegance of the performing. As several members of the company played the two-stringed *erhu* fiddle, the Chinese lute *pipa*, and percussion, the team of six actors went through their exacting athletic paces.

They wore lush customs of silk brocade and thick, masklike makeup. Each color of the rainbow was represented and each color signified something. In this national opera art form, everything—the colors, movements, and sounds—spoke a language.

Red—bravery. Purple—sincerity. Black—robust warmth. Blue—savagery. Yellow—arrogance. Green—instability. Orange—old age. Gold—the gods. The lines on each face meant other things. Usually, the more simple the lines, the kinder the character. The more lines, the more complex the character. Even each different kind of beard meant something (three-part beard—honesty; short moustache—rudeness; thin moustache—comedy).

And that's just on the face. Colors of the costumes also imparted information to the audience. Red was for the aristocracy; crimson for barbarians; blue for honest men; green for virtuous characters; white for the aged; black for aggressiveness; pink and turquoise for young and old women. Each hue could mean something different, and there were subtle subdivisions in each color—just as the meaning of a word changes when pronounced differently.

But the actors were not just puppets performing rituals where their costumes and makeup did all the talking. There was an encyclopedia of acting style. Zhang had showed Daremo at dinner to try cheering him up. There were twenty kinds of laughter alone. The slightest movement is significant. He showed how he could change the same laughter's meaning with the position of the lips, the eyebrow, the hand.

He changed the mirth from surprised to shy to hearty to despairing to worried to frightened in the space of seconds. It was a masterful display he continued on stage. Every character had specific movements that signified different things with every part of their body. They imparted emotion and character simply in the way they moved.

"Autumn River" was the tale of a nun who falls in love, then hires a boatman to take her downriver to her man. Daremo remembered it. He had seen part of it in the Kowloon amusement park. Zhang Meng played the old boatman and Shih Miao played the lovesick girl.

"Stealing Silver" featured Li Lianjie and Hung Donglian as Xiao Qing and a guardian god. The wily Xiao outfoxes the guardian to escape from the vaults of Qiantang county with many riches and much gymnastics. The pair dazzled the audience with their tumbling skills.

But even their display couldn't match the masterpiece of Yuen Baio and Fu Liang doing a lively version of "At the Crossroads"—one of the most popular and requested stories. Baio was the virtuous Yang Yanzhao, and Liang was the slippery Liu Lihua. Mistakenly thinking each other a threat to a mutual friend, they have a magnificent battle in a darkened room—even though the stage was infused with light.

Each man had a long sword and there were tables and chairs in the pitch-black room, leading to a spectacular display of choreography and timing. Every portion of the body and every prop was used in a continuing spiral of delightful surprise.

Just when the audience thought there was nothing more the actors could do with a particular situation, they built on it again and again until the people were shrieking with laughter.

By the end of the night, Daremo was smiling proudly behind the animal makeup Zhang had lovingly applied himself. Both men still stayed in makeup to hide their identities. Daremo had helped with props and costumes, and at the close of the evening's entertainment, he helped pack up.

"Next stop, Tunxi, in Anhui province," Zhang reminded everyone. "We have to perform there tomorrow, so we'll have to drive all night."

The cast groaned but kept working diligently. "How far is it?" Daremo asked as he passed the director, lugging a heavy metal pole with rusting, old klieg lights attached to it.

"A little over three hundred miles," Meng said. "Practically straight up." Daremo merely nodded. He said nothing there, or for most of the night ride through Jiangxi. He sat in the chair as Zhang slumbered. He gauged the trucks' average pace as thirty-five miles an hour. At that rate, they would reach their destination in about eight hours, not counting stops. He kept track of the time with his mindwatch.

The caravan stopped only once, in Shangrao, so they could relieve themselves and stretch. During the break, Daremo removed peasant clothing and a wide, nearly flat peasant hat from the costume truck. He secured it in Zhang's vehicle. When the caravan reached the border of the two provinces, the sun was coming up. Daremo quickly changed into the peasant outfit and prepared to jump out the back. By the time the trucks stopped, he'd be well into the underbrush.

"Wait."

Daremo resisted the urge to jump anyway.

"Please."

He paused, and turned to face Meng, who was getting out of bed. The overweight, bearded man went to the corner of the enclosure, where his personal belongings lay in a pile. He moved the material out of the way and carefully dislodged a small square opening in the truck floor.

The noise, dust, and gas fumes from the undercarriage invaded the flatbed as Zhang reached in. He sat up on his knees, holding an automatic pistol. It was standard Chinese Army issue—a 7.62, Type 51.

"Please," the man repeated. "I want you to take this."

If Zhang was an Em-en, this would have been the time to kill Daremo. He would have taken the gun out and shot the ninja where he stood. Even if Daremo had dodged and jumped, the trucks following could have run him down. Instead, Meng simply held the gun out to the round-eye with both hands.

"Please," he said for the third time. "I want you to have it."

Daremo said nothing, his expression blank. He walked forward and took the gun by the barrel. "I know your way is fraught with danger," Zhang said.

"Come on, *lao pengyou*," Daremo chided. "Nobody talks like that."

Meng almost laughed. "Very well, then. I think you may need it more than I."

Daremo put the weapon under his shirt, in his pants waistband. "You may be right." He walked to the lip of the back opening. He wanted to jump. He meant to jump. But he just stood, watching the road go by.

He felt. He felt something. He felt emotion.

He saw their faces: Alan Pierce, Rick Aponte, Stu Richards, Paul Schonberger, Larry Oshikata, Willie Palmer, Bill Hale, Bill Stone, Bob Bourgeau, Steve Ellroy, Irv Arocho, Mike Barnes, Ken Murphy, Scott Harmon. Plain, average names. Plain, average people on the surface. Beneath the surface, no one is average.

He saw the others' faces: Yuen Baio, Fu Liang, Shih

Miao, Li Lianjie, Hung Donglian, Cheung Chiang, Zhang Meng, and the others. He owed them nothing. He should have felt very little for them.

He had gotten used to only feeling something for those he loved or those he killed. But to ninja, all feelings, all emotions, were torture. It made sense that they should only torture themselves over the extremes, over the "important" people.

I have experienced something of human nature.

I know.

I have seen these people live. I have seen them go to work every day, eight hours a day or more. I have seen their wives, their friends, their children. I have talked to these people. I have shared all their dreams.

Does it bring you peace? Serenity?

Pause. Yes. Strangely, yes. It shouldn't, but it does.

Their ways are aimless. They are just living. They don't seek anything more than to fit into their environment, their man-made environment. They exist only within God's physical framework. They ignore the laws of nature to prosper—to work, to marry, to survive.

They seek not perfection. They seek survival.

Yes. That takes an extraordinary will.

Don't think that way. They would laugh at you.

They would, but just to survive that way is an achievement.

What way?

Holding on. Without giving in. Remaining honorable, mantaining morality in the face of the insanity around them.

Insanity? What insanity?

Everything. The vehicles that belch poison. The poison they put in their bodies. The poison they put in their minds.

Like this?

Touché.

Don't be foolish. What would you have them do? Question endlessly? Be like you?

Rob banks?

Very good. You got me back.

They live their lives with nobility, never admitting or realizing it.

If they did, they wouldn't be noble, would they?

No, I guess not.

So what are you trying to say?

Maybe that as stupid as it sounded, I wanted to say it. I had to say it.

It's time for the big, stupid concepts.

I'm dying, so I'm allowed?

Correct.

Here it is, then. I admire them, but I do not aspire to them.

You are ready.

Am I?

Yes.

To die?

Yes.

Sigh. Pause.

Well, let's get this show on the road, then.

Daremo jumped out of the back of the truck.

12

Ten thousand steps.

Huang Shan. Thousand-Mile Eyes had said it. Huang Shan. Mount Huang.

Moshuh Shan. The queen mother of the the West had said it. Magic Mountain.

Kao Fei had said it. Mount Huang, the Magic Mountain—headquarters of the *Moshuh Nanren*.

How did he know? How do you know where the FBI is? How do you know where Daremo's ninjutsu school is? It's common knowledge. Not man-on-the-street common knowledge, but people who wanted to find the *Moshuh Nanren* knew where to find the *Moshuh Nanren*.

Up ten thousand steps carved in six thousand feet of rock. Mount Huang cut into the sky like a huge finger pointing to heaven.

Death waited at the summit. It had been prophesied.

But understanding waited there, too. It had been promised. Daremo had walked for days to reach this spot. He had walked through mud-walled villages and emerald-green rice paddies. He had walked six hours from the last town to reach the base of the mountain.

He stood now, one foot on the first stair. The steps went into the misting morning clouds. He considered his options for the last time. If he did not climb, he would die in ignorance. He had already been shot. He sat dying on the other side of the clouds.

He stood at the base of the moutain, frustrated and upset. He knew not why he had lived. He knew not why he was dying. He did not understand the disturbing images, the memories, the dreams, the nightmares. He couldn't stop existence without knowing. Eternal torture: true hell.

So he would walk up the stairs. He would go to his death . . . to understand. He would not die in confusion.

As he ascended through the mist, he descended into hell. The rocks became the gods. The wizened pines became the demons.

"I have waited for you," said Yenlo Wang. "Welcome to the kingdom of Yama. You will be judged."

"I have lost all hope, Yue Lan," Daremo professed. "I am ready for judgment. What is my hell?"

"There are hundreds in the underworld," said the featureless god. "Have you no family who would pray for you?"

He thought of the dead ones. He saw the massacred parents, the slaughtered wife. He recognized the mutilated Oriental woman from his previous vision. That was her—Brian Williams's wife. He thought of Rhea Tagashi, her love, and then her decision to kill him.

"None."

"Have you no friends who would do good deeds to ease your may in the underworld?"

Daremo thought of Archer, one-armed Archer. He had been poisoned in San Francisco, losing him the use of his left arm. He had been poisoned again in Israel, in the Negev Desert town of Bar Sinai—losing him the arm itself. He did not know where the man was now. But he knew that Rachel would be with him. He knew she would see him through the amputation. He, Daremo, could no longer claim Archer's spirit as his own.

"For the crimes against the man and the woman, I forfeit my friend's deeds," he said.

"Be certain. The tortures here are beyond any tortures you know." There was no doubting the ruler of this hell.

"I cannot claim his deeds for my benefit."

"Already you have eased your punishment. You are a man of honor."

Daremo remembered his murders. He remembered all the people he had killed with his bare hands. He remembered the victims he could not save.

"I am not. Do not insult me."

"You are a man of pride," Yenlo Wang decided. "Consider; your hell will be of honor and pride. Think of the perversion of those sins."

"I seek not to lessen my torture, King Yama. I seek understanding only."

"Then climb on, no man. Climb on. You shall live out

your remaining time as a hungry ghost, doomed as shadow without substance. All food and drink will turn to ashes when it touches your lips."

"I have not eaten or drunk for days."

"You will not, ever again. You will know the mists of Avici, which will rise up and turn your flesh to dust."

"I shall expect it, then, King Yama. I yearn for it."

Daremo walked on. Yenlo Wang, ruler of the underworld, stopped. He was soon far behind the human. "Goodbye, no man. I shall miss you."

Daremo walked on. For the record, climbing Huang is like walking up the steps of the World Trade Center, only the stairway to Daremo's hell was on an eighty-degree angle.

An old man with a golden headband and a crutch walked alongside the ninja. "You have come," said Li Tiequai, the first of the eight immortals. "Are you prepared?"

"I do not think so. I can no longer distinquish reality from fantasy."

"Ah," said the crippled old man. "But can you distinquish which is the reality and which is the fantasy?"

Daremo looked to the immortal. "I see," Li said. "There is still time." He stopped by the side of the stairs and lay a leaf on a limpid pool. "Step on this. If it holds your weight, you shall enter Tao."

"It is too late," said Daremo, his pace not flagging. "I must go on."

But he turned back to see the old man joining a man with a sword and a fly whisk in the shape of a horse's tail, a man with a fan made of feathers, a man riding a white donkey, a judge, a young man carrying peaches, another young man with a musical instrument, and a woman with a lotus. The eight immortals watched Daremo disappear in the fog, then returned to the queen mother.

"Go no further!" Daremo heard from above. He looked up to see a creature with bat wings, an eagle's beak, and clawed feet.

"I must," Daremo told the thunder god. The creature roared its displeasure.

"Go no further!" shrieked a woman who held mirrors in each hand.

"I must," said Daremo to the lightning god. She hurled bolts from the mirrors, which ripped out lines of shale from the jagged rock formations all around him.

"Go no further!" cried an old man carrying a closed leather bag.

"I must," said Daremo to the wind god. The old man opened the bag, nearly knocking Daremo down the steps. He was slammed to the rock face, his eyes blinded. But somehow, he kept walking.

"Worship us," the gods demanded.

"I shall. I do." The storm subsided, and Daremo continued on.

The storm had been real. The visions could have been real too, for all Daremo knew. For all he knew, they were his mind's representations of real threats. Chinese military guards. *Moshuh Nanren* operatives. They could have been waiting on the stairs to kill him or stop him—and he saw their fights as conversations with Chinese gods.

Without stopping, he took the gun from his waist-band. He removed the magazine. There were still eight bullets in the clip. He returned both the gun and the ammunition to their places. He looked at his hands. He had not fought, to his knowledge. There had been no guards—if he had a shred of sanity left.

Laughter.

He heard laughter in his brain. A barking laugh, then some low, chuckling mirth, then another laugh.

No guards.

What?

There are no guards here.

Daremo shook his head. Whatever was now inside his mind was beyond description. It screeched, it rolled, it communicated in ways beyond words. It combined images and sounds and feelings to create a comprehension that was way beyond human communication of any sort.

No matter how subtle and precise the Peking Opera, no matter how amazing the achievements of science, medicine, and the arts, these seven words exceeded the limitations of the most advanced human. Beyond Daremo himself.

I need no guards. You have seen my guards.

The feeling was exact and unerring. By rights, the mountain should have been crawling with security forces. Instead, he had seen taunting Chinese deities. The echo of the images that were left in his mind communicated that those deities had not been created by Daremo. They had come from outside his own imagination.

Time was no longer operative. He sat on the top of

the mountain, between unconsciousness and death. And he walked up the stairs, his legs on automatic. No matter what happened inside his head, his eyes had a direct link with his limbs. He continued walking.

He was in San Francisco, Connecticut, Africa, Iran, Turkey, El Salvador, Israel, Hong Kong, and China at the same time. His life was not passing before his eyes. It lived in his mind. It did not move in sequence, it simply was all there. Daremo could not understand it. He did not recognize it. He was seeing it as one lump thing from the outside.

Come. Come to Hui.

He was Hui. He was the "one" the Figure in Black had referred to. He was the man—more than a man now. He was the being who had discovered the eye to the inner mind, the rest of the mind.

Daremo knew Hui and Hui knew Daremo instantly. The bridge was made. The doors had been opened long ago and stayed open. This is who Daremo had come to stop. This is whom he had come to kill.

Kill? How? How will you kill me?

He did not know. He could not. For if he did, Hui would know as well.

Instead, he climbed the stairs. He climbed for three hours. He climbed through the ceiling of white, which became the sea of clouds. He climbed into the cold wetness. He climbed to the top of the "erected lotus bloom."

He climbed to the room without walls, floor, and ceiling. To his back was a large rock, the fingernail that jutted higher into the heavens. On all sides of the circular apex was nothing. No fence, no bannister, nothing. Just clouds for as far as the eye could see. The crown of Mount Huang was a tiny island on a sea of clouds. Before him was a courtyard covering fifty feet. Beyond was a stone temple.

It was the same as almost any other. Its ceiling was green. It was squat and wider than it was tall. It looked to be an empty room. It stank of excrement and refuse. There were two steps leading up to a small stone porch. On the flat granite of the porch sat the mystic Hui.

He was naked in the cold air. His skin was the color and texture of aged parchment, more brown than yellow. His hair was white and grew off his face and head to his lap, to cover his sex organs. He was thin, frightfully so. Curiously, his finger- and toenails were short.

Hui had discovered his inner mind. He had experimented on himself to develop the brain-control weapons the *Moshuh Nanren* had used. He had opened his mind into a body and society that were not prepared. His appearance and his home might seem incredible, but it was because it had to be.

Hui could not exist in a hospital or a traditional house or a laboratory. He lived inside his own skull. Daremo remembered his own agony when he had gotten too close to Archer and Rachel's love. He had felt their emotions. In a city or town, Hui might have physically exploded from the pressure.

I eat and I eat and I eat and I eat, but I grow no stronger in body. The metabolism can't keep up.

You must stop. Daremo imagined his words were like baby noises to Hui's mind.

I am your future.

It couldn't be. Daremo ignored the sensation. He had to keep the mind flow going. He had to find a way to destroy the creature.

Where are the others?

There are no others.

Daremo was amazed. Hui's powers had a dark side. He could not keep certain feelings and emotions to himself!

They deserted you!

Their minds flowed together. The sensation was as one.

The Moshuh Nanren *was hired to help pro-Mao revolutionaries turn China back from the Four Modernizations. When the diversions were destroyed in El Salvador and Israel, the Plan was cancelled.*

Postponed.

Hui's mind roared. Daremo fell to his knees, nearly fainting. He dropped to all fours, choking saliva drooling from his mouth.

The Plan is postponed.

Stop! Daremo begged.

No no no. I must control minds. I cannot live among others unless their minds are mine are mine are mine . . .

He was not crazy. More the horror. He was thinking truth. If he controlled their minds, he could survive. The Plan was no longer important. Daremo had been instinctively right. Finding and killing Hui was all-important.

The Moshuh Nanren *want you dead*.

No. They seek to save face. *Convince the Mao forces to go forward with the Plan*.

The Moshuh Nanren *assisted me to reach you. They used me as your assassin because they didn't want to risk suffering your fate*.

No. You are a child. You know nothing.

It was all a fantasy. It had to be. None of this could be real. Everything—the gods, the Iran robbery, the endless slaughter—paled in the face of this unreality.

Die!

Kill me, then. Come forward and kill me. It can be done. KILL ME.

Daremo stepped forward. Three men appeared from inside the temple. They wore comfortable, normal clothing. They wore down jackets. They held Type 64 and Type 43 sub-machine guns.

Daremo's weapon was out from under his shirt instantly, but it was too late. He managed to kill one of the guards with his first shot, but the other guards ripped up the stone behind him with 7.62 bullets. Most missed him, but three went into his lower torso.

Daremo sat down. Hard. His whole body shook as his ass hit the moss-covered rocks.

Please, he begged. I don't want to go through this again.

He watched through dimming eyesight the surviving guards standing on either side of Hui. He distantly heard them laughing at him and congratulating themselves on fooling the round-eye ninja. The *Moshuh*

Nanren guards were there at all times, in case anyone escaped Hui's mindlock.

The mindlock. Daremo remembered it well. It had been used on Rachel Assaf. It was a wall in the brain. The subconscious was held captive. The conscious was controlled in a limited fashion. The *Moshuh Nanren* had devised a machine that could speed the process.

He heard the Cantonese of the guards. "We killed the ninja. Even the vaunted Liu Chia could not accomplish what we have done. We killed the white ninja."

Daremo's soul raged. Where was the understanding here? All he felt was the death.

Suddenly, Hui was standing. He was pointing at him.

"No!" he heard the words. He saw the image in Hui's mind.

It was an image of his own torso. Above the wounds, above the open shirt, there was a thin cord tied loosely around his neck. And on the cord was a simple circle of jade.

The guards died. They simply fell over as the *shurikens* slammed into their heads.

Right on, Daremo cheered. That's the way to kill them, baby. Let me have a little satisfaction before I go.

Leaping before his fallen body was the Figure in Black. He had climbed up the *other* side of the mountain—the sheer face of Mount Huang—to reach the apex. He had jumped from the jutting crag to stand before Daremo, facing Hui. In his hands was a sword embedded in a hilt of wood, a sword held in the *Jigoku Aisatsu* position. Hell's Greeting.

Oh my God!!!

Hui's curse followed Daremo's, but it was beyond verbal translation. It was a spasmodic, bone-cracking vision of rage and hate. It swirled together and blasted from his mind like a blunt arrow shot from a cannon. It exploded through Daremo's forehead, ripping his mind in two. It cut through the visions and memories to the mindblock.

It exploded, destroying the wall. Realization rushed into his consciousness.

He was not Daremo

Daremo stood before him.

He was Scott Harmon.

It was amazing how stupid his name sounded and how unimportant his life seemed now.

Harmon's cry of fear and terror was beyond anything he had done before. He was dying twice, two times over. He was losing two lives.

This was the understanding, the terrible understanding?

I am sorry.

What have you done?

I had to reach this point. I could not defeat the guards and Hui. I had to have a diversion.

I was your front?

The Moshuh Nanren were trying to convince the Planners to continue. They are in Japan at this moment, trying to destroy the minja as show of their ability. This was the time. It was the season. I had to do it now.

What did you do to me? How?

Mindblock. Your memory was behind. My memory

was in front. You believed you were me. You became me.

How? How?

Your mind was empty. You life was ruined. I found you (in the gutter).

The phrase was too clichéd for Daremo to complete. Harmon fed it into his own brain. He remembered. He remembered the fire.

He remembered the face, the figure in the fire—the placid face that had come after Rhea, Rachel, Michelle, and Brian William's wife. It had been the face of *his* wife, Scott Harmon's wife, Elaine.

It had been the face of the woman who had died in an early morning fire with her two young children.

I am sorry.

You keep saying that.

You entered Hong Kong with your own passport. You threw it away because I could not chance you seeing your picture and breaking the mindblock. You never looked into a mirror. You never saw your own face. You thought it would be my face.

How did you know?

I tested you. Disguised as the Figure in Black, I trained you. I gave you the tanto *blade.*

Harmon laughed in his mind.

I look like you, fine! But you! You! What about your face?

How could you get here with your face?

He knew the answer as he laughed and asked. He suddenly saw the Figure's body. It was heavy, wide.

Daremo took off the black hood. Beneath was Zhang Neng's face.

I could change my weight, I could grow a beard, I could alter the focus of my eyes to require glasses. But I could not control my eye's shape.

It was all true! Heng's wife and child *had* been killed in the drug trade! His wife and child had been Brian William's, Brett Wallace's, and Daremo's wife and child!

Harmon groaned, on the edge of death. He called out. He called to Michelle.

I did not control her. She was your own. He promised Harmon that.

Brains don't lie, right?

She was yours.

An unforseen circumstance?

I "felt" her rape. I sent the emotion to you so you could find her.

Michelle.

Love.

Darkness.

Eternity.

White light.

Death.

Daremo. The real Daremo.

He stood before the mystic Hui. His sword was up. The guards were dead. Scott Harmon was dead. He couldn't move.

The bridge between their minds was locked. They struggled inside their heads.

Laughter.

You do not understand.
I have not understood longer than you.
We fight.
We fight until one of us discovers a new weapon.
You will not win.
Laughter.
You cannot control your own mind.
No.
Soon it will be beyond your comprehension.
No.
Autism.
No.
Catatonia.
No.
Your brain is beyond your own mind's understanding.
No.

Mindlock. Daremo stood, paralyzed. He felt nothing and everything at the same time. There was no tangible pain, but the effect was electrifying, soul-searching. An invisible hand gripped his skull in a vise. He was a statue that could still think, but he didn't dare. No thoughts. He had to use everything inside his skull to counter Hui. If he did not, he was certain the mystic could enter... control... destroy.

Hui stood up. He smiled. He was fighting Daremo to a standstill but had enough left of his mind to control his muscles. Slowly, agonizingly slow, Hui walked toward Daremo. As he walked, he raised his arm, his fingers bent into claws. He walked toward Daremo, reaching for the sword.

Bravado. He sent an image to Daremo's mind's eye—

of Hui taking the sword, holding the ninja in the mindlock, and plunging the blade into the living heart.

He could do it. Daremo knew he could do it.

Daremo ran.

Claustrophobic horror.

Bulging, vein-covered, sacklike walls, all dark crimson and purple. He sank into the floor. His hands sank into the walls. He was nearly choked by the stench, blinded by the acid mist.

The halls twisted into insane, impossible shapes. He could hardly move. It was like running on a cloth-covered lake. With each step, he sank. He had to crawl, twist, pull, and step again.

Daremo!

He couldn't do it, but he had to. He let go of part of his mind. He felt it falling away from him, sideways, out of sight—as if thrown over the horizon.

Where are you?

He could run better now. He slithered down the pulpy hills, rolling, crashing into the walls, falling into the slimy, overstuffed, sausagelike mattresses.

Come back!

He choked, screaming. he whimpered and cried tears. He was beyond fear, beyond terror. He was alone. He had almost no time.

He was not *there*.

I'll destroy you! I will destroy you!

He could feel it. He could feel the tearing. He could feel entire handfuls being torn out.

Laughter, Die! Die! Die!

He was being torn apart there. Here it was dark and it was empty. So horribly empty.

Don't question; accept.

Face it, fight it, go on.

Don't look for it. *Be* it.

Don't hold on.

Daremo transferred completely. He forced his being into the dark, empty place.

It was unnatural. It was unholy. It could not be. It was not. In the eye of the serpent, it had not happened.

But the one signal went out. Daremo had been in and out at the same moment. The spark—the living spark—that had been created by the impossibility put the message out.

Hui was standing directly in front of Daremo. He had the sword in his hand. The sword rose. The point was over Daremo's heart. Hui smiled.

Scott Harmon shot him.

13

Harmon's finger had spasmed. The finger around the trigger of the automatic still in his hand contracted.

The dead man fired the gun. The bullet went into Hui's heart.

He stopped smiling. He fell back. He died.

Who's to say what the mind is capable of?

Brain dead. Doctors can't pinpoint it. The energy lives, on they say. Can you believe that? Can the brain's energy continue after the heart has stopped? How long does a man live after death? Is there a soul?

There are no answers to those questions. Only these answers: Harmon's soul left his body empty. He was an empty machine. New owner—Daremo. In the driver's seat, aim, fire, and out.

Back to his brain, hoping he still had one to return to. Was it Daremo's soul that made the trip? Was it his aura? Was it energy. The same energy that created all supernatural phenomena?

The gods saw it like this. Hui collapsed. Daremo nodded, fell to his knees, then to his face. The day went by, and then the night.

Daremo rose at sunrise. The Mount Huang clouds glowed glorious colors. Eternity stretched all around him. Now this was real. This was no psychic bullshit. This glory existed. He was in China. He was on earth.

He could think.

He could feel.

Hell, he could stand.

Daremo leaned over and took his sword from Hui's dead fingers. He stood up painfully. He looked all around. There were the five corpses. There was God's magnificence stretched all around him. There was the army of his dead.

They stood all over the misshapen rocks, looking down on him as if he were in the Coliseum.

Two *Moshuh Nanren* guards were there, in the front row. And Hui. Scott Harmon was not there. He was gone forever.

The sun was coming up. Its edge appeared from the clouds, like a laser disc slicing through cotton.

Ki-chigaino.

Scott Harmon's family had died in a fire. Daremo returned to the devastated man and used him terribly. Even after death, he used him. He had nothing to be proud of. To kill an insane mystic—a man who no longer had the ability to communicate with human beings, a man who was really no longer a threat to the world—he had played god.

Ki-chigaino.

But there he was—alive, able to think clearly, without psychic interference, among nature's consummate beauty. It all was possible in the light of this. The mountain, the sky, the sun. Who dare say there was no God in the face of this?

Ki-chigaino.

Daremo was happy. He stood among all the people he had murdered, deliriously happy. He carefully raised his sword to them.

It's silver blade caught the sun. Beams of golden light stretched from horizon to horizon. A band of light streaked into the sky, going forever.

Slowly, purposefully, the army of dead raised their hands. They applauded their messiah.

The jade circle lay on Harmon's motionless chest.

27 million Americans can't read a bedtime story to a child.

It's because 27 million adults in this country simply can't read.

Functional illiteracy has reached one out of five Americans. It robs them of even the simplest of human pleasures, like reading a fairy tale to a child.

You can change all this by joining the fight against illiteracy.

Call the Coalition for Literacy at toll-free **1-800-228-8813** and volunteer.

Volunteer Against Illiteracy. The only degree you need is a degree of caring.

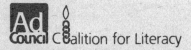

Ad Council Coalition for Literacy